Cyrus The Persian Messiah
© 2016 Mason Balouchian
Library of Congress Control Number: 2017904210

Hard Cover Edition: ISBN 978-0-9905973-4-6
Paperback Edition: ISBN: 978-0-9905973-2-2

Publisher: Mason's Publishing
Casselberry, FL 32707
mason@adgraphicstudio.com
www.CyrusThePersianMessiah.com

Cyrus The Persian Messiah
Cyrus the Great

He never knew in the distant future, far away from Persia, the greatest superpower on Earth would establish a democratic dominion based on his Human Rights Charter.

Mason Balouchian

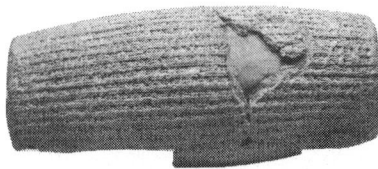

The Cylinder

Mason Balouchian

A breeze through the fragrant growth,
Across the oceans of time and space,
Carries the whispers of the Father:
Behold, young children of Persia,
The spirit of Cylinder rises again —
Liberty! Liberty! Liberty!

Contents

The Cylinder v

Acknowledgments 1

Preface 3

Prologue 5

Chapter 1 9

    Interpretation of a Dream 9

Chapter 2 13

    The Birth of Cyrus 13

Chapter 3 17

    The Shepherd's Son 17

Chapter 4 19

    The Game 19

Chapter 5 21

    The Encounter 21

Chapter 6 27

    Dining with the King 27

Chapter 7 31

    House of Achaemenid 31

Chapter 8 35

    The Persian Dominion 35

Chapter 9 43

    The Battle of Pasargadae 43

Chapter 10 51

    Susiana 51

Chapter 11 59

    An Inspiring Dream 59

Chapter 12 63

    The Slaves of Babylon 63

Chapter 13 75
   The Battle of Pteria 75
Chapter 14 81
   The Battle of Thymbra 81
Chapter 15 87
   The Siege of Sardis 87
Chapter 16 95
   An Expedition 95
Chapter 17 107
   The Messiah 107
Chapter 18 115
   Human Rights Declaration 115
Chapter 19 123
   The Massagetai 123
Chapter 20 127
   The march against Massagetai 127
Chapter 21 135
   An Abandoned Camp 135
Chapter 22 139
   A Conspiracy 139
Chapter 23 143
   The Final Confrontation 143
Chapter 24 147
   The Death of the Father 147
Epilogue 151
Renaissance 153
List of illustrations and photos: 155
Coming Soon 157
Novelettes, and Short Stories on Kindle 159

Acknowledgments

This is an opportunity for me to thank all those who helped me to achieve the honor of writing and publishing this book. On top of the list is my mom, who placed the first book in my hands when I was in 2nd or 3rd grade and told me, "here, this is a book remaining from your father's library. The people believe whoever reads this book would become a traveler." Of course, at that time, she was referring to my brothers who had gone travelling for different reasons, yet the magical statement took me on a fascinating journey of turning pages in an endless search to find the answer to, 'what happens next,', the key element in every successful story. She did not know that one day, I would write these words from America, a distant land across the world that is the ultimate destination for seekers of freedom.

Next on the list is my family, without whose enthusiastic persuasion I would have been stumbling in the rough terrain of writer's block, until who knows when I would have finished the last chapter. And last, I would like to thank Hope for her amazing touch. She did a great job and truly made my work better.

Preface

Working as a freelance tour guide during the '90s, I visited the tomb of Cyrus the Great on many occasions. During these visits, I learned about this fascinating figure in detail. Later in 2011, I decided to write his story in a dramatic form because I thought that Cyrus, as the original architect of the Human Rights, had not been given the attention he deserved. I had to research many elements such as characters, events, battle scenes, dates, etc. to come up with the story you have in your hands as a historical fiction. It is historical because the major plot is based on facts published by Greek historians or philosophers. It is fiction because characterization, dialogues, internal thoughts, scenes, and sub-plots are my own creation. These elements have been dramatized for story captivation, but they reach the same conclusions recorded by reliable sources such as Herodotus, Xenophon, and other historians and writers. The Persian resources were, unfortunately, burned during Muslim invasion of Persia in 7 AD.

I wrote this book with three objectives in mind. To mold the scattered pieces of Cyrus' life in a coherent story that projects the highlights of his accomplishments. To create an attractive right-to-the-point dramatic form that includes dialogues, narratives, and scenes in right proportion in order to entertain and avoid boredom. And finally, to present a story to all readers who wish to know about the true architect of the Human Rights and how he affected the lives of more than 40,000 Jewish slaves in Babylon and many other oppressed nations during the Persian historical period.

Prologue

Cyrus the Great[1] was the founder of the Persian Empire during the ancient historical period. The word Persia originates from Pārsa, a tribe of Aryans who lived in Iranian central regions. At present, there is a province in that area called Pars. In ancient times, however, the Greek historians referred to the whole empire as Persia.

The original inhabitants of this land descended from an ancient civilization dating back to about 7000 BC. Pottery remains, excavated at different archeological sites, indicated evidence of these civilized societies. Aryan tribes from around the Caspian Sea had been gradually migrating into the Iranian Plateau for thousands of years. In early 2000 BC, the migration took a faster pace. Upon entry, they divided into three major groups and settled in different areas—the Persians in the center, the Medes in the west, and the Parthians in the east. They founded diverse systems of government in these regions.

The Persian belief system during this period was Zoroastrianism. Zoroaster[2] came from the eastern part of the country. There are controversial arguments about his date of birth, among which 660

---

1   576 – 530 BC
2   Ancient Iranian philosopher.

BC sounds the most reasonable[1]. He established his philosophy on the existence of Ahuramazda[2], the Spirit of Goodness, and Ahriman[3], the Angel of Darkness. This credence was later employed by Gnostics, Sufis, and Travelers who sought spiritual elation by con-

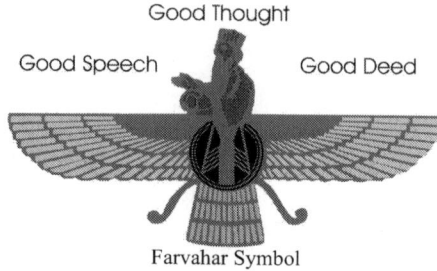

Good Thought

Good Speech   Good Deed

Farvahar Symbol

trolling the domineering self[4]. His teachings included three major principles, leading man to salvation: Good Thoughts, Good Speeches, and Good Deeds. His doctrine became the motto of the Persian Empire, established by Cyrus the Great.

Following the foundation, the Persian Empire initiated a progressive lifestyle that lasted 1200 years. It included three major empires and 83 years of Seleucid Rule[5]. The epoch began with the issuance of the Charter of Human Rights by Cyrus the Great[6], which

1   "...before the Arab invasion (642 AD), no Persian doubted the date of birth and death of Zoroaster because all precise and authentic historical information were registered in four thousand volumes of books in Ctesiphon and other libraries in Iran. But after Arabs invaded Persia, they burnt all the historical records..." (ZARATHUSHTRA; The First Monotheist Prophet: by Nurbakhsh Rahimzadeh)

2   God.

3   Lucifer.

4   Ego. Forces of darkness in human.

5   Achaemenid Empire (550-330 BC), Seleucids (330-247), Parthian Empire (247 BC - 224 AD), and Sassanid Empire (224-642 AD).

6   Hundreds of baked clay tablets excavated in Persepolis, now in the museum of The Oriental Institute of University of Chicago, indicate compensations to workers from different parts of the world. These vouchers and invoices prove that workers were paid wages and slavery was not practiced in the Persian tradition. Besides, there is no mention of the word slavery in Gathas which means Zoroasterians did not believe in such improper practices.

caused the durability of the Persian rule for a long period of time.

Cyrus' main concern was to promote the modern visions recorded on the tablet, known as Cyrus' Cylinder[1]. His name is mentioned in the Old Testament[2] as the deliverer of the Jewish people. Xenophon, the Greek historian and philosopher, refers to him as "the ideal ruler." In the introduction of his translation of Cyropedia[3], Larry Hedrick [4] writes, "What Moses was to the Israelites, Cyrus was to the Persians. The Persians regarded him as the *Father*, the Babylonians as the *Liberator*, the Greeks as the *Law-Giver*, and the Jews as the *Anointed of the Lord*. Plato praised him as the *Model of Enlightened Monarch*. The Shah of Iran regarded him as a *Historical Paradigm of the Persian Dominion*. Thomas Jefferson, the president of the United States, studied Cyropedia, and in a letter to his grandson recommended him to read the book in his Greek studies.[5]

Whatever his mission, Cyrus was a practical man who led a relatively short and simple life, yet achieved great results in leadership and Human Rights. He reigned 29-31 years and established an empire stretching from the Indus Valley in the east, to Macedon and Thrace in the west, and to Egypt in North Africa. He respected the right of the people to practice the religion of their choice and

1 A clay cylinder created in Babylon recording Cyrus' Human Rights Declaration.
2 ...Who roused from the east him that victory hails at every step? Who pre...Thus says the Lord to his anointed, to Cyrus, whom he has taken by his right hand to subdue nations before him and strip the loins of kings, to force gateways before him that their gates be closed no more: I will go before you levelling the heights. I will shatter the bronze gateways, smash the iron bars. I will give you the hidden treasures, the secret hoards, that you may know that I am the Lord. (Isaiah 45:1-3)

3 Xenophon's *Cyropedia*, a glimpse of Cyrus' character or the education of the ideal ruler.

4 Xenophon's Cyrus the Great: the arts of leadership and war/edited with and introduction by Larry Hedrick.

5 Among the classical Jewish sources, besides the Bible, Josephus (first-century Romano-Jewish scholar) mentions that Cyrus freed the Jews from captivity and helped rebuild the temple. He also wrote to the rulers and governors that they should contribute to the rebuilding of the temple and assisted them in rebuilding the temple. A letter from Cyrus to the Jews is described by Josephus.

observe their own traditions. His success lies in a clever constitution of an administration that favored the interest of the citizens in his empire. He was mostly inspired by the teacher of purity, Zoroaster, whose simple message carried the substance of love and perfection fantasized in a place of ideal excellence known as utopia. His magical message was Good Thoughts, Good Speeches, and Good Deeds. The man who said: "To battle darkness, I do not draw my sword, I light a candle."

Our story begins in Ekbatana[1], capital of Medea. The Medes have established a confederation with the Persians who rule Anshan. Astyages, the King of Medea, has given his daughter in marriage to Cambyses I, the Persian King of Anshan.

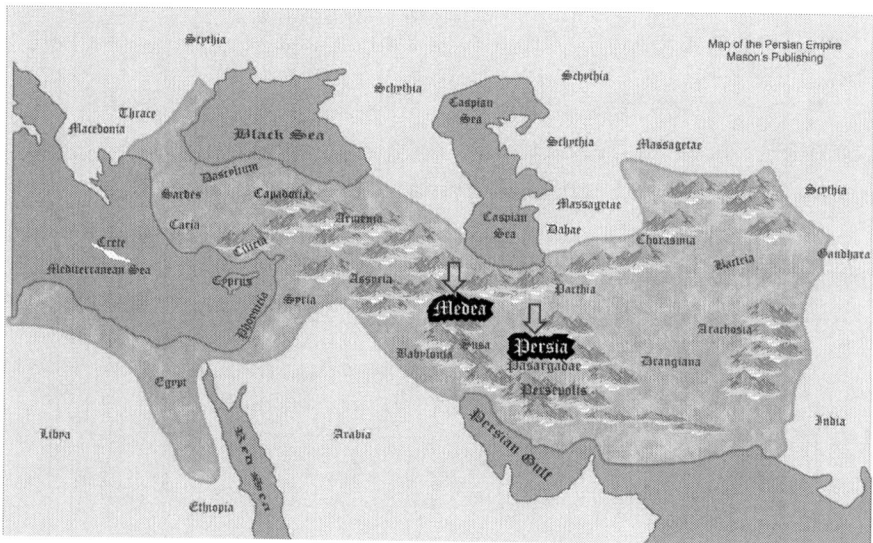

Ekbatana and Anshan about 600 BC

---

1 Presently called Hamedan.

Chapter 1

Interpretation of a Dream

The chill from the stone bench and the silence of the reception palace made the interpreter restless. He stood up and walked to the window. The silhouette of cypress trees in the garden looked menacing against the gathering dusk. *It must be an important dream*, he thought. He heard footsteps in the hallway. The guards moved to attention. The chamberlain appeared at the gate and invited the interpreter inside. At the Hall of Audience, King Astyages waved the chamberlain out, and they were alone. The man looked at the king with apprehension.

"I had the strangest dream," Astyages said, "I thought you can put an end to my concern."

"Long live the King! What is the nature of that dream?" the interpreter answered.

"Well, my daughter, Mandane—she is in my palace and seems to be playful. All of a sudden, she faints and falls down on the floor." He stared at an unknown spot in the distance. "At first, it is a small plant growing out of her belly. Then, it grows to the size of a tree, so big that the branches crush the walls of my palace and spread as if to fill the skies and oceans."

He retreated into a long silence. "This dream—I have seen repeatedly for three nights," he finally said, looking at the interpreter in anticipation.

His voice echoed in the hall. The interpreter could see shadows moving far away among the columns. *Ears of the interior household.* He was deep in thought trying to find a way out of the terrible situation. He could not tell lies. He knew his life was in danger.

"My lord," he said in a troubled voice, "Your daughter is going to give birth to a child. This child will become the king of kings. He will rule the whole world. He will be the king of earth, water and air."

There was a pause again. Even the shadows did not move. He did not dare to look Astyages in the eyes.

"What about the collapsing walls of my palace?" Astyages asked in a threatening voice.

"Long live the King," the interpreter answered, "he will succeed you and rule over the land of the Medean Empire." He emphasized the word succeed involuntarily.

Astyages looked at him with fury. "Succession happens peacefully. Do not try to fool me with your choice of neutral words."

"My lord, I beg your grace to say it."

"Granted!" Astyages said, turning his back.

"He will defeat you in a final confrontation and establishes a new empire," the interpreter whispered with quivering voice.

The thrust came so rapidly that the man did not have time to fear. He lay dead on the floor.

The child must die, Astyages thought. *I have to keep my dream a secret until Mandane returns to Ekbatana. She will give birth to her baby here in Medea.*

Chapter 2

The Birth of Cyrus

In the secret grotto under the palace, Harpagus was shivering at the thought of the task ahead. It was about midnight. He had been waiting there for a few hours. Astyages had once appeared and encouraged him to stay and wait. He was loyal to the king, yet could not convince himself to kill the baby. *That is cruel—who would kill his own grandchild? Astiages is going to regret it. If it is a boy, he will be the Prince of Persia. My plan is perfect—even if discovered, I will have logical reasons to explain it.*

He heard footsteps on the stairs. It was Astyages holding a small bundle in hand. The baby had been wrapped in soft cloth. Astyages threw the bundle into his hands as if getting rid of some abomination. Harpagus felt the warmth of the baby's tiny body and reached to look at its face. Astyages held his wrist.

"You should hurry and carry out the task," he whispered as if fearing to be overheard. Then he climbed a few steps, but stopped for a moment and turned back. *Oh, I wish I could take a look at his face one more time.*

Harpagus noticed the doubt in his eyes. "Anything troubling you, my lord?"

"No, go now," he waved Harpagus away. "Bring me the news when you are done."

The full moon sprinkled azure blue light on the wasteland around the hill. The gruesome silhouette of the tower of silence brought fear to Harpagus' heart. There were no horses in the stable down the hill. *Mitradotes has not arrived yet,* he thought. He left his horse in the stable and started climbing the ramp. After a while, he stopped to catch his breath. Below his feet and in the distance, he could see the glimmer of lights in the village. Far away from the tower, he heard the trotting of a horse. *That must be Mitradotes.*

Remains of two towers of silence in Yazd Province, Iran

He climbed up the ramp. Inside the tower, the moon was casting dark shadows of unknown possibilities against the high walls. He moved toward the stone platform in the center. The vultures on top of the walls stirred in anticipation. He laid the small bundle there. The vultures did not smell death. The stone was cold and the baby started crying. Harpagus heard footsteps coming up the ramp and moved into the shadow.

A vulture landed beside the baby. Harpagus moved forward swiftly, slew the vulture and pulled it into the shadow. *I have to wait until Mitradotes discovers the bundle by himself. I will report that I left the baby at the Tower of Silence for the vultures. It won't be a lie.*

The noises from the entrance made him withdraw into the shadow.

Mitradotes entered the tower and moved toward the platform. He paused there surprised by finding the crying baby. "Oh lord, this is a miracle," he said picking up the baby. He left his own bundle there instead. Harpagus moved out of the shadow.

"Greetings, Commander Harpagus," said Mitradotes sadly.

Harpagus pointed at the bundle on the platform with questioning eyes.

"Oh, commander, my wife gave birth to a dead son,"he said looking at the baby on the platform.

Harpagus reached for the baby in Mitradotes arms and revealed his face. "Well, I have good news for you,"the blessings of Ahura Mazda—A beautiful baby sent for you from the heavens."

Mitradotes looked at the child with disbelief.

"Does anyone know that your child was born dead?" Harpagus asked.

"Not yet, Commander Harpagus; she delivered two hours ago, only her mother was present."

"Listen, Mitradotes, now that you found this baby, raise him as if he is your own child. Bring him up as if your boy were alive. Tell no one of your own baby's fate. Here he is—healthy and beautiful."

Mitradotes hugged the baby with affection. "Oh, lord, what a beautiful creature—but whose is it?" he asked looking back at Harpagus.

"This must remain a secret between you and me," Harpagus said, "I will tell you who he is in due time; no one must ever know that your child was born dead; if anyone finds out about the origin of this child, you and your family will be in great danger. Go hastily now, and make sure your wife and mother-in-law understand it."

Harpagus mounted his horse. "Name him Cyrus; I will return to see him soon; make sure he is taken care of very well."

"He will be worthy of his name," Mitradotes said, "you know, in our tongue it is Kurosh, a shepherd—he will be like me."

Not exactly, Harpagus thought, *he will be The Shepherd—one who will lead his people to a great destiny.* Then he rode off and left Mitradotes in wonder.

Chapter 3

The Shepherd's Son

Cyrus was raised in Mitradotes' household and under supervision of Harpagus until he was five. He was a genius learner and displayed noble behavior. Mitradotes was a leading highlander and served as the royal shepherd. He spent time with Cyrus regularly regardless of his occupation. He was a wise man and tried to teach Cyrus all he knew. His family took great pains to educate their children.

When Cyrus was five, Mitradotes taught him horsemanship. Harpagus arranged for other training sessions. He rose early in the morning and appeared at the training court with the other boys. They exercised running, throwing spears, and shooting with the bow and arrow. When seven, he was taught to ride like a warrior. First he learned ordinary management of the horse. Later, as he grew older, he practiced shooting arrows while the horse was in full gallop. Then, as a young Mede, he learned to jump on and off the horse at high speeds.

He was educated by his parents, Harpagus, his tutor, and mainly through observation. Cyrus became familiar with the conviction of the believers, good thought, good speech, and good deed—the three fundamental principles of Zoroasterians. His father always taught him to speak the truth. "Truth is the essence of all virtues. Doing good to others is not a duty, it is a joy and increases our own health and happiness," he would always say.

His tutor taught him moral lessons through epic poems. In these poems, the gods, heroes, and heroines were set to battle against demons and villains. Afterwards, Cyrus was required to give an account of the story or recite the poem. The most important practice, however, was observance of the truth. Philosophy, politics, and history were other subjects of his interest. Harpagus had much information about the two latter subjects and did not miss any opportunity to teach him. He learned much about the migration of his ancestors to Medea and Persia. Harpagus also trained him the manner in presence of kings and courtiers.

Cyrus exhibited an incredible ability to absorb knowledge. Soon he exhausted his tutor by bringing up complex questions about philosophy and human social behavior. His tutor encouraged him to turn his attention to observation if he thirsted for more knowledge. He spent most of his private time in reading and contemplation. By reviewing the teachings of Zoroaster, he gradually perceived the world around him more profoundly. He discovered that observing the rules of simplicity, honesty, and fairness attracted great alliance.

He started to practice these principles in his daily relationships, and discovered their power. Wonderful things began to happen as he practiced keeping a positive attitude. The more good thoughts he formed, the more charm he radiated. Even older people were attracted to him and appreciated his wisdom. His fame as a wise, young man soon spread across the Medean territory.

Chapter 4

The Game

Cyrus had to issue a wise verdict. One that was not influenced by his ego. The boy was the son of Commander Artem-Barce fighting in the Assyrian front. Cyrus noticed that the boy had been extremely jealous of his leadership. In this game, the boy had been acting as the commander of the enemy's army. He had lost the fight, was arrested, and brought before Cyrus for judgement.

"We forgive him for his venture against our forces. He has been acting out of patriotism, which is to be praised. Release him and let him go free," Cyrus commanded, waving his hand.

The boy jolted his shoulders from the grip of the guards, faced Cyrus in close range and said, "you are taking the game and your role too seriously. Have you forgotten that you are the son of a shepherd?"

It was only a game, but now the boy had made it personal. "Seize him," commanded Cyrus. The guards clutched at the boy's shoulders again and thrust him down to his knees.

"I admire you for your courage during the battle," said Cyrus calmly, "I forgive you for your boldness to talk ungraciously in our presence, but I have to punish you for insulting the shepherds."

Then he turned to the crowd of boys acting as courtiers and said, "Who raises the lamb for your tables?"

"The shepherd!" They shouted.

"Who provides the cheese to eat with your bread?"

"The shepherd!" Everyone cried.

"And the wool for your clothes?"

"The shepherd!" They answered.

Silence fell. Cyrus looked the children in the eyes and said, "Shepherds are good citizens—as blacksmiths are, as farmers, shoe-makers, educators, and other citizens are. They are all warriors on different fronts. They fight against the greatest enemies of humanity: poverty, ignorance, and indolence."

"Put him to the bastinado[1] for insulting our citizens!" He shouted, pointing at the boy.

---

1   A punishment consisting of beating the soles of the feet with a stick.

Chapter 5

The Encounter

Cyrus was riding to Ekbatana along with his father and Harpagus. In spite of their worry, he was calm and happy to be visiting the king. He had seen the palace from a distance many times, and he was excited to be going inside on this occasion. As they approached the city, the magnificent palace on top of the hill came into view. Along the way, Harpagus educated Cyrus on how to conduct himself in the presence of King Astyages. Harpagus did not want to be seen with them in the town, and therefore he parted when they engaged in conversation with the guards at the palace gate.

After a short interview, the guards escorted them to the reception palace. Cyrus was thrilled by the beauty of the hallways, high ceilings, and quality of drapes hanging high and loose on the windows. Every few trayas[1], there were built-in depressions where guards stood at attention; they were dressed in beautiful Medean costumes—pants and short skirts. They were holding long spears and had short swords at their waists. The spears did not touch the floor; they held them in the air. That was the sign of their total readiness

---

1   Ancient Persian unit of measurement equal to about one foot.

for action in case of a threat.

They waited in the reception palace until the chamberlain arrived and led them inside through the most beautiful garden Cyrus had ever seen. The floor of Central Avenue was covered with baked bricks of various shades. On either side, flower beds were filled with violets of differing colors along with other exotic species he had not seen before. Farther away, he viewed rows of evenly-distanced cypress trees decorating the sides of the path. Beyond the cypress trees, there were square orchards uniformly spaced out and allocated to a variety of fruits such as apples, persimmons, and citrus. Between the square orchards, there were small avenues covered with a velvety lawn that was constantly sprayed with water from unseen sources within the grass. Occasional rose bushes in the grass added to the beauty of the garden. On either side of the pathway, clear water was running in shallow gutters and gardeners were tending the vegetation.

In the royal court, King Astyages, nobilities, royal household, and other courtiers were present. Astyages stared at Cyrus for a long while. He had already heard about him from different people. A skinny boy with a sharp nose and long black hair. His penetrating eyes studied him briefly before kneeling. *What a charismatic young man,* thought Astyages, *and the resemblance....*

Mitradotes knew about the customs of courtiers and had already trained Cyrus to behave like one. They kneeled before the king and remained silent. Astyages rose from his thrown, came nearer and looked more closely at Cyrus. Then he addressed Mitradotes.

"I have heard of your son's wisdom. What is his name?"

"Cyrus, my Lord," said Mitradotes.

And his name...this could be just a coincidence, Astyages

thought.

"There is a complaint about him from my most valued commander."

Mitradotes kept silent.

"Cyrus has dared to put the commander's son to the bastinado."

"Long live the King," Mitradotes said, "and hail, General Artem-Barce. The children were just playing a game."

"Let me hear his account of the incident," Astyages demanded.

He turned and looked at Cyrus with curious eyes. "What do you have to say, young man?" He felt some affection for the boy.

Cyrus did not look up at the king as his father had instructed him. *Do not look him in the eyes—keep your head down and answer in a low voice. He is ruthless—and one wrong move can trigger his anger.*

"In this game, my lord, I had been elected as the king. I had to observe the dignity and determination of a king," he said with confidence.

"Besides, when my own right is at stake, I can forgive, but not the right of other citizens. I could not forgive that."

The crowd was stirring.

"What right of others?" Astyages inquired.

"The right of our citizens—he insulted the shepherds by looking down on them. Soon he will be among the elites. What guarantee is there that he will be just to his subordinates and humble cit izens? My role in this game, my lord, demanded that I make a wise judgement, which I did. He must have been punished to learn his lesson."

Mitradotes was shaking from fear. The crowd had a sigh of admiration for the boy to talk so gallantly before the king.

Astyages was lost in his thoughts. *The striking resemblance, his noble behavior, and most of all, his courage. He could not be the son of a shepherd. He behaves like a prince. He must have some noble origin. I must investigate.*

Everyone was looking at Astyages in anticipation. He was absorbed in his inner debate for a few moments. Then he looked up at the crowd and said,, "I want to be alone with Mitradotes and Cyrus."

The audience was excited as they left. Finally, they were alone. Astyages told Mitradotes that he knew the boy was not his son. Paralyzed with fear, Mitradotes told him he had found the child in the tower of silence. He only skipped part of the truth by failing to mention his conversation with Harpagus. They had already agreed to say just part of the truth in case they were forced to uncover Cyrus' origin.

Astyages had his guards keep them in custody, summoned Harpagus, and inquired about the fate of his grandson. Harpagus explained that he could not convince himself to spill the blood of a Medean prince and did not want to betray his loyalty to the king either. He said that he was also afraid the king might later become regretful and punish him for killing his grandson. Therefore, he left everything to fate and laid the child at the tower of silence. He added that he had witnessed from a dark corner that Mitradotes had found the child while leaving his own dead child there. He added that he had been monitoring the child being raised by Mitradotes. Then he kneeled before Astyages and demonstrated his loyalty by offering his head to pay for his disobedience.

Moved by his allegiance, Astyages forgave him. He also admitted that he had grown fond of the boy and did not wish him dead any longer. Of course, he did not reveal his grudge for Harpagus, who had placed him in such a difficult situation. Then he sought advice of the interpreters to see if the threat still existed. They believed the prediction no longer prevailed because the child had already been elected as a king among the children. Astyages had been challenged when his grandson issued a command to punish the commander's son and if the king approved of Cyrus' decision, he would have admitted defeat and fulfilled the prophecy.

Chapter 6

Dining with the King

The meat had an unpleasant taste. Harpagus cut another piece from a different plate and brought it to his mouth with his stick. It tasted the same. He pushed the meat around his plate and busied himself with the rice. He had been surprised by the invitation—dining privately with Astyages was an unusual privilege. He had dined with the king before, but only during public festivities. *He is trying to express his appreciation for finding his grandson alive,* Harpagus thought. This was an occasion to get even closer to him and share the concerns of the middle class.

The dinner continued in silence with occasional courteous remarks. There was a golden bowl still uncovered in the center of the table.

"How did you like the meal, Harpagus?" Astyages asked.

"Very good food, my lord—I enjoyed it."

"Now, I want to reveal to you what you ate," Astyages said with a hideous grin.

"I thought it might be some new game, the meat tasted unusual," Harpagus answered.

"Yes, indeed. It must be surprisingly unusual to you."

And while the servant uncovered the bowl, he continued, "My dear Harpagus, take a look inside the bowl to see what you ate."

Harpagus went closer and looked inside the bowl. He felt as if he were struck by lightning. He was confused. His heart was bursting with sadness and sorrow. Blood rushed to his upper organs. His stomach had been rejecting the food since his first bite. His first reaction was to reach for his sword, but he remembered that he had been disarmed when coming inside. Besides, what good would it do him? He would just get himself killed without feeling the satisfaction of revenge. He was absorbed in fury and internal argument and not aware of his surroundings for a few seconds. Finally, logic overcame and he got control of himself.

"Punishment for those who betray my orders," he heard Astyages say in the background.

Inside the bowl, there was the head of his son looking at him with horrified eyes. The first shock had now passed. Then he was occupied with the thought of revenge—a clever reaction that could guarantee his vengeance. Crying inside, he planned his next move.

"Oh my lord, what a wise decision to punish me in the most original fashion," he said, kneeling before Astyages.

"I submit to your will, and I am ready to offer my own head to minimize the king's wrath."

Surprised at his loyalty, Astyages held his shoulder and made him stand. All his anger had diminished by Harpagus' gesture. He hugged the man and told him that he appreciated his loyalty and was sorry for what happened to his son and wished him to continue serving in his army. Harpagus who had achieved his purpose in disarming Astyages, kissed his hand and went home to mourn the death of his son.

Astyages sent word to his daughter and son-in-law informing them of Cyrus' appearance and imminent travel to Persia. The royal court celebrated the event and the Persians cheered the arrival of the crown prince. Soon, Cyrus became a popular figure in Persia.

Chapter 7

House of Achaemenid[1]

Cyrus had been listening and watching for hours. From his hide-out in the tree, he could clearly see the path leading to the pond. Every feeble sound attracted his attention. He did not miss even the slightest noise made by the leaves falling in their passage to the ground. He heard the distant rustle of crushing dry leaves while the deer approached. There were inflexible rules to join the Sword Bearers. The animal must not be hurt in any way. He had to catch it with bare hands. It was a matter of pride. "When hunting, you have to be cunning and deceitful," his father had said, "especially when you hunt a lion. A deer, however, is difficult to catch when it's pursued. You must, therefore, take it by surprise." His success in this test would advance him one step closer to the leading position he was going to claim among the young elites.

The deer looked young, light-weight and ready to run away. Cyrus was determined not to make the slightest mistake. His plan was perfect, and he knew it would work. The riverbank below his feet was soft with grass. The deer had to pass that narrow path—

1   The Persian nation contained many tribes one of which was Pasargadae. Achaemenid was a clan of Pasargadae from which Cyrus the Great sprang.

an easy prey, he thought. It moved closer, but stopped and looked around by some instinctive reaction, as if it felt the approaching danger. He had chased deer many times before, but this one had an unusual behavior. It seemed to feel some dreadful presence. Cyrus held his breath and did not move a hair. It was almost at the desired spot now. Just a few more steps and he would have it by the neck.

He was getting ready to jump when he felt the beastly breathing. It was close, for he could feel its warm breath. The hair on the back of his neck stiffened. Something was creeping on a nearby branch. The deer had reached the desired spot now. He did not want to miss the opportunity. In mid-air he got a glimpse of the mountain lion. Perfect timing. It had jumped exactly at the same time, as if challenging Cyrus for the prey. As they neared the ground, Cyrus gained advantage because the deer jumped to the left and, for a short moment, he used its body as a support and managed to land on the back of the mountain lion who came down exactly where the deer had been a moment ago. Surprised and scared, the beast ignored the deer and leapt toward the path leading to the creek. Trying to escape from the persistent rider, the lion jumped up the cliff on its right. Cyrus lost his grip on the lion's mane and fell as the beast climbed. He broke his fall using his hand, but hit his head on the rock, slipped down the cliff, and fell into the water. He passed out for a brief moment half-immersed in water. As he came to, he spotted some movement from the center of the pond. A woman was rushing toward him. He had not fully recovered yet, and thought his imagination was playing a trick on him.

The beautiful woman was naked. She had black hair that reached her waist. Her eyes were two perfect jewels of emerald green. She held and dragged him out of the water. Her breasts brushed against his face. She left him on the grass, leaned on him and put her ear on his chest. Then she held her hand near his mouth to make sure he was breathing. Cyrus did not want to open his eyes because he thought that the dream creature would disappear. When she was certain the danger had passed, she went away around the bushes. Cyrus opened his eyes and sat on the grass. His hands and shoulder were bleeding. Moments later, she returned in a short, brown tunic. Cyrus realized it was not a dream, and she was real. He admired her as she approached.

"What heavenly creature are you?" Cyrus asked.

The girl laughed aloud. "I am just a regular girl."

Cyrus pressed on the staff she had brought for him and tried to stand while she provided support for his other hand.

"You are an angel to me," he said, while resting his hand on her shoulder. It felt warm.

"I was shocked watching you ride on a mountain lion. Only the legendary heroes and deities ride on predators."

"And only Anahita[1] emerges from the water to help the heroes," Cyrus answered, bewitched by her striking beauty.

"You deserve a title far beyond a Sword Bearer, son of Cambyses—rider of the lion," she said, wiping the blood from his forehead. Cyrus looked up—a few people were approaching. His father was riding before them. The woman got ready to depart. "You didn't tell me your name," he asked before she disappear among the bushes.

"My name is Cassandane. I am the daughter of Pharnaspes," she said and swiftly ran away before the riders arrived. Cyrus knew her father. He was the head of a noble clan with a good reputation among the Persians. Later, Cyrus married her. He loved and cher-

1   Goddess of water in Elamite mythology. Angel of water in Zoroastrian Philosophy.

ished her throughout his life. He always reminded her how he had
fallen in love with her when she saved him from the lake.

Chapter 8

The Persian Dominion

Cyrus had proved to be a military and political genius. His father appointed him to the throne when he was just turning 18. He organized the most skilled army ever known among the Persians. He was a benevolent manager and established an accounting system to reward his permanent military members on an exact payday. Likewise, he started a system for the public to register in his army for wartime and go through paid training periodically in order to be combat-ready. Cyrus was preparing to announce independence from the Medean government.

He was continuously in touch with Harpagus through a very reliable agent and sought his advice to choose an appropriate time to announce independence. Harpagus assured him of his total loyalty and promised assistance if there was a battle. He also advised Cyrus that he had some high-ranking allies who vowed to join him in revolting against Astyages.

When Cyrus lived in the Medean royal palace, he got acquainted with his nephew, Barzon, a swift and tough fighter. They had also been friends in their training camp before Cyrus' true identity was known. Cyrus admired him for his courage and skill. He was very keen with the short sword. Once, they ventured at the northern borders of Medea during a hunting trip. It was right after sunset and they were returning to their camp when they were attacked by two Massagetae. They were so quick that no one had ever captured one them alive. They always attacked at night. Cyrus confronted one of them who fled after receiving a few slashes. Barzon, however, cornered his opponent and did not give him a chance to escape. The man displayed much courage fighting with Barzon. He was small-er but faster and soon found out that he was no match for Barzon who used his skills to play with him by advancing fast and crushing him with a lunge. Then he retreated and let him push forward. He took advantage of the Massagetae's power to fling his weapon out of his hand. Then he retreated again to let the man pick it up and charge once more. Barzon was finally through with the exhausted Massagetai and ripped his heart with a final blow. They knew that the savages were committed to removing their dead from the scene of conflict once the battle was over—they were the most dangerous at this time if interfered with. Cyrus and Barzon left the dead body there and fled before swarms of the savages arrived.

Thereafter, Cyrus and Barzon became good friends. When Astyages was sending Cyrus to Persia, he suggested that Barzon go along and serve as Cyrus' personal bodyguard. Cyrus and Barzon both agreed. Later, before their departure, Astyages had talked to Barzon and told him that regardless of his service to Cyrus, he must remain loyal to the clan and the Medean court. He had detected a gruesome intention in the king's tone of voice.

Barzon felt great allegiance toward Cyrus, because he thought of him as a wise and just leader. He believed that Cyrus would lead the Persians and Medeans to glory—a greatness not acquired by bloody wars but through gentle ways of peace, and benevolence. His devotion to Cyrus had gained him the position of serving as his personal guard—the most trusted office in the Persian royal court. Cyrus had never doubted his loyalty and liked him as a true brother.

The news from Anshan was not pleasant to Astyages. Cyrus' popularity and support was increasing in his court. There were rumors that Cyrus had declared independence. Astyages had to act fast and have Barzon complete the job Harpagus had failed to fulfil years ago. Thus, he sent a secret message to Barzon, ordering him to murder Cyrus. He threatened to kill his parents if Barzon did not obey his orders.

The message did not weaken Barzon's loyalty toward Cyrus. He had learned the principles of conducting a good life from Cyrus. He knew that good thought would be put to practice through good deed. This was an occasion to test the purity of his thoughts. He was obligated to his parents and faithful to his lord. Being pure in his thoughts and deeds, he could not serve two masters. There was no trace of uncertainty in him. He was determined to support Cyrus and remain loyal to him. The salvation of the two nations was in Cyrus' survival. He also thought of a plan to save his parents.

The guards moved to attention as they heard the squeaking of the small door contained in the gate[1]. Cyrus emerged from inside and walked toward the hallway. He was in the center of the lobby when he heard Barzon from behind.

"I need a word with you, my lord," he sounded hostile.

"All right, Barzon, but can that wait for I have to meet with the delegation from Medea? They are heading for the reception palace, as you know," Cyrus answered.

---

1   Small door installed in the palace's huge gates for informal traffic.

"It cannot wait, my lord. In fact, I want them to witness the imminent event."

Cyrus turned back, frowning. The guards were all ears.

"Fine, what is so important that cannot wait?" Cyrus enquired.

"My lord, I have to admit that I have never stopped admiring you as a great leader. But now your ambitions are conflicting with that of King Astyages," he paused, "I have been ordered to put an end to this hostility. I have no solution other than to challenge you in a fair fight until one of us dies," he finished unsheathing his sword.

The guards quickly moved forward to protect Cyrus. He stopped them with the wave of his hand.

"You have been a good friend of mine all these years," Cyrus said. "You have saved my life several times. How could I ever think of fighting you to death, my friend?" He slowly moved toward Barzon." Astyages is a sick man. You do not have to be loyal to him. You know I am his heir. By serving me, you are being loyal to your clan and your country."

The delegation was now approaching through the hallway on the other side of the lobby. They were heading for the adjacent reception hall. They were about to witness an unusual event. They stopped and watched from a distance while escorted by the Persian guards.

"Forgive me, my lord, I have to meet my obligation," Barzon said, charging forward.

"I fight you with regret, my friend," Cyrus said. He unsheathed his sword and pointed it at Barzon.

Barzon charged again. The swords came into contact and sparks flashed in the air. They fought aggressively. A few slashes and thrusts were exchanged and then the excitement transformed them into two angry fighters challenging in an arena. Cyrus was familiar with Barzon' tactics. He had trained himself to counter his tricks. During a man-to-man fight, Barzon always fought with short sword in one hand and dagger in the other. He was very skilled in handling the two weapons with both hands.

After many exchanges, exhaustion gradually appeared in both opponents. Throughout the fight, Cyrus noticed signs of hesitation in Barzon. Once, Barzon charged with his dagger from the left while shielding his right side with the sword. Knowing the tactic, Cyrus blocked Barzon' lunge with the sword in his right hand and gained more momentum by turning on his left foot. Yet that would put Cyrus in a difficult position because his right hand had just been engaged in defense and the next blow was coming from the same side, where his hand was still motionless and not able to tolerate the hard blow.

Cyrus had practiced a counter-attack for this trick in secret. He shifted his weight on the right foot, dodging his opponent's blow and delivering a surprising strike behind his sword. He was certain that it would remove the sword from Barzon' hand, and he would have the advantage to strike. He completed his move, landing on his right foot with a lot of momentum ready to deliver the final stroke. To his surprise, Barzon made an unexpected move, and his chest was now the target of Cyrus' thrust.

That was a suicidal move, and Cyrus knew that Barzon would not make such a mistake unless he deliberately wanted to expose himself to a deadly blow. He avoided the fatal thrust by loosening his grip on the sword. Then he turned and struck the sword out of Barzon' hand. Now he was aware of Barzon' intentions. He had no time to waste. With the handle of the sword in his left hand, he gave Barzon a hard blow behind the neck and hurled his unconscious body a few feet away. In the distance, the spectators were relieved. Cyrus knew Barzon was unharmed and merely had a negligible wound on his chest. He had the guards remove the body, and whispered to them to keep Barzon in a remote cell and take care of him. He told them to make sure everyone knew that Barzon was dead. Then he attended the reception palace to negotiate with the Medean delegation. The next day, he arranged a respectful funeral for Barzon to make sure the news of his death reached the Medean court by the delegates.

Before announcing independence from the Medean rule, Cyrus established a council assembled from the elites of the royal court. Educators, artisans, military commanders, and other professionals were present. He included young and old in the assembly for he believed the young would make the group more flexible and dynamic while being inspired by the wisdom of the elders. He set the mission of this council to seek ways of establishing justice and equal rights for all people living in the Persian territory.

He knew that the success of a secure and lasting empire depended on staying away from tyranny; that a vast empire must be ruled by a small, self-sustaining system of governments, loyal to the central office of the emperor while remaining popular among their own local people. It would be a monarchic confederation like the Medean Empire where he was born and brought up. There was, however, a major difference. He vowed not to run this system like Astyages. All governors would have to be accepted and liked by the majority of their own people. In such a system quick communication was very important. Also, a successful military operation was seriously dependent on fast and efficient logistics. Thus, he ordered the construction of courier houses along the major roads every four parasang[1] to keep fresh horses. The couriers riding along these roads switched horses at these stations. They could carry messages

1   Ancient Persian measure of distance approximately equal to six kilometers. The distance a horse could walk in one hour.

to distant destinations in a short period of time. He also demanded the construction of caravanserais[1] along the major roads at one day travel distances where travelers could rest and recover overnight.

Striking coins from gold and silver to facilitate trade was another one of his innovations. Barter had become inefficient. Traders did not want to readily convert their profit into other forms of merchandise where they sold it. Coins gave them more flexibility to seek their favorable commodities elsewhere.

He also came up with the idea of keeping the public informed of the current national news. A group was assigned to employ stone masons to carve reliefs of important events on the rocks along the royal road, so that the people traveling through the country could find out about the ongoing events, such as recruitment of soldiers, victories of the state, and national festivals.

He organized a royal army into regiments of a thousand each. Ten such regiments made a division. He assembled a division called Royal Guard Immortals, because their number should always stay the same. As members died or left service for other reasons, they were replaced by freshly trained soldiers. He used a system of colors, mostly blue, purple, and yellow to identify different units. During wars, he employed the tactic of placing the shield-bearers in the front. They carried large, rectangular shields and short spears. They formed a wall with their shields and the archers fired from behind to soften and divide the enemy forces. Then he launched his shock attack by cavalries that were lightly equipped with short swords. They were aggressive, fast, and very effective.

Every soldier was paid a monthly salary and those who worked as contractors were required to issue invoices recorded on clay tablets. Every year when the auditors inspected the treasury department, these invoices were required as evidence of the expenses. The

1 Roadside lodges where travelers could stay overnight.

commanders of all division were also required to issue vouchers to document monthly payments to the soldiers and officers. As Cyrus strengthened his fundamental capabilities and stretched his dominion, the interests of the Persian dominion came into conflict with that of the Medean Empire.

Chapter 9

The Battle of Pasargadae

The chamberlain announced the presence of the Medean tax collectors outside the gate of the reception palace. Cyrus granted the audience. The delegation had met Cyrus on previous occasions. They knew what would come next. As usual, the king would greet them and ask the chamberlain to provide accommodations and food so that they could rest a few days while the treasurer prepared the annual tax and toll. This time, however, they faced a completely unexpected scene. They seemed to have confronted a ghost. Barzon was standing beside Cyrus as if he had never died. Some of the group members recalled witnessing his death at the hand of Cyrus during a previous visit.

"He is not a ghost," Cyrus said breaking their trance, "and his parents are safe living with him now. Astyages does not deserve your loyalty," he continued, "you know he would kill you all if you return empty-handed. You will have a day to decide if you want to serve the Persian court. Of course, we will arrange for Astyages to think you have been taken as prisoners for your families' safety. Otherwise, you will be free to go. Barzon will discuss the details with you," he concluded looking at Barzon.

Within the following year, there were occasional confrontations between the Persians and the Medes until the ears of Cyrus reported that Astyages was preparing a sizable army in order to attack Persia.

*****

The magnificent sun was rising from behind the eastern hills of Pasargadae. It sprayed golden rays on the Persian army positioned in the plain. The royal tent had been erected on the hill at the southwest outlet of the Pasargadae plain. Cyrus was watching the army from there. The plain was surrounded with low hills on all sides. It was like a vast, natural arena. There were two outlets: one behind his army in the east side and the other in the west where the Medean army was expected to arrive. Flag holders had taken up positions on strategic hills to transfer his commands to the army.

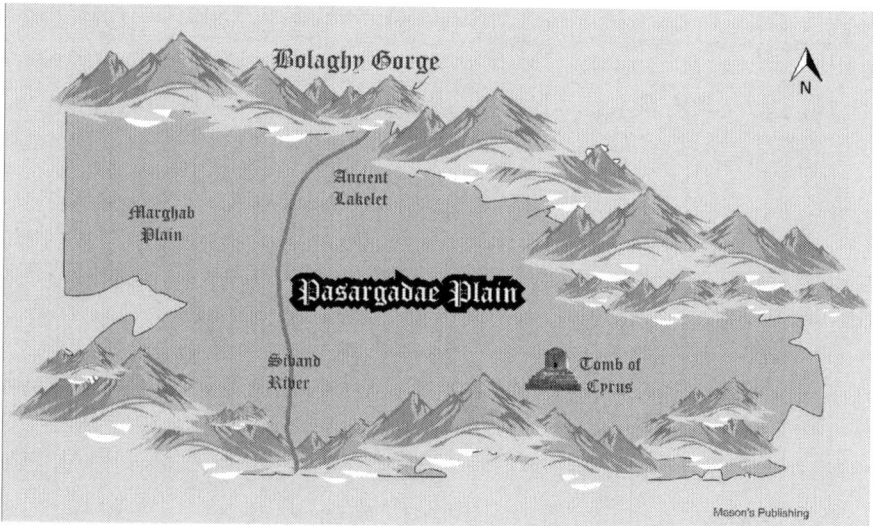

Cyrus knew that Astyages would not march his army inside that natural fortress unless he positioned his watches on the surrounding hills, which had already been occupied by the Persian forces. He would therefore position his army in the open plain and face Cyrus there. Cyrus moved an infantry division out in the open plain and kept part of the cavalry division behind the east hills for support.

Soon, the sound of the Medean army marching toward Pasargadae was heard. By noon, they were positioned against the Persians. Three cavaliers separated from the their army and rode forward. Cyrus sent Barzon and two other cavaliers to negotiate. They rode forward and met the Medean delegation halfway between the two armies.

"I see that you survived the battle with Cyrus." Barzon recognized Harpagus among the three riders. He dismounted his horse and came forward with open arms. Barzon returned the kindness.

"Listen, Barzon, we are going to advance with our infantry. All commanders have agreed to take Cyrus' side," said Harpagus.

"When we approach your army, our troops are going to turn and face Astyages. The cavalry is going to follow suit from behind. Astyages is going to be defeated and overthrown. Our generals are ready to announce loyalty to Cyrus. They are all fed up with Astyages' cruelty," he added.

"The whole nation is ready to accept Cyrus as heir to Astyages. Go back to your army now and get ready for a bloodless transition," concluded Harpagus mounting his horse. He was going to have his revenge. *I want to see Astyages' reaction—defeated and miserable,* he thought, riding back alongside his companions.

As the commander of Astyages' army, Harpagus led his troops in a well-planned maneuver and joined the Persian army. There were cheers among both armies as they exchanged friendly greetings.

Only a few groups remained on the Medean side. A single rider separated from that small camp and stopped midway between the two armies. There was a stirring among the Medean soldiers. They recognized the man from far away. He was Commander Artem-Barce who was unusually tall and rode a black horse.

"Astyages is sending him for a last challenge," said Harpagus.

Cyrus nodded. "What do you suggest we should do?"

"We must ignore this gesture and capture Astiages while we can," Harpagus answered, "he is the most cunning of all when desperate."

"Well, he is my grandfather. Granting him his last wish is not going to hurt anyone."

"He must have some trick up his sleeve again," Harpagus said; "do not trust him, he is like a wounded snake now—he would bite anyone in his way before giving up."

"Why don't we listen to his request and decide what we want to do," Barzon said.

"Well, I know Astyages better than all of you. Whatever he has in mind is neither heroic nor honorable. He is using Artem-Barce to carry out his evil intention," Harpagus answered.

Cyrus was thinking. Finally, he looked up in agreement. "Harpagus is right. We should refuse the challenge. Astiages has no choice. I do not see the point in risking even one life that can be spared."

A group of five people, led by Barzon, met Artem-Barce midway between the two armies. Astyages had sent a sword and a word for Cyrus: *This is the sword of my ancestors. I will be honored if Cyrus kills me with this sword.*

Barzon carried the sword and the message back to Cyrus. "He is ready to surrender, but he has one last wish. He wants to be killed by the sword of his ancestors and in the hand of Cyrus." Said Barzon.

Harpagus looked at the sword suspiciously, "There must be a trick to this. No one should touch the blade. It could carry a deadly poison."

"Let me try it on an animal by giving it a slight slash," Barzon said, removing the sword from its wrap. His grip lasted only a moment. He dropped the sword and held his palm for everyone to see. Three drops of blood had appeared on his palm.

Harpagus picked up the sword with care, not touching the handle, and examined it. There were three tiny needles embedded in the center of the jewels on the handle.

"He has poisoned the handle. I knew he had a hideous plot. He intended to kill Cyrus and reclaim the crown again, for there was no one else here who could claim it. With this simple trick, he could have won the war and added Persia to his kingdom again."

Barzon felt weak. His legs could no longer support his body. He fell down on his knees. Everything was blurry. The moment he sensed the sting in the palm of his hand, he knew he would die soon. Astyages had finally brought his wrath on him. The realization that he had not succeeded in killing Cyrus, however, brought a smile to his face. He knew that his death would result in Astyages' defeat. When the medicine man arrived, Barzon had already been paralyzed. He was aware of the events around him, but he could not move a finger. The medicine man opened his pouch and produced a small bottle of a brownish syrup. Cyrus had Barzon' head on his lap and looked sad. The medicine man lifted Barzon' head and poured some of the syrup into his mouth. The bitter potion went down his throat. He forced a smile at Cyrus and died.

Astyages surrendered with little resistance. He appeared on the hill and addressed both armies.

"...The Medeans and the Persians are cousins," he said, "our ancestors came from the same clan of the north leaving behind the savagery of the wolf land. We came here to seek peace, pastures and farms. We are from different clans but the same origin and now is the time to join forces together. That would make us stronger against our enemies.

The warriors cheered in agreement.

"There are threats from the empires of the west. Soon they will be pounding on the walls of our cities. Cyrus, my grandson is the one to stop them before they invade our lands. He shares the blood of the Medeans and the Persians. He is wise, courageous, and a great leader."

The warriors cheered as he paused to recall the prophecy following his dream. Then he raised Cyrus' hand and said:

"He will be the king of land, air, and water. Submit to his command for he will lead you to a great destiny."

The warriors' cheering gradually diminished as they started pounding on their shields with their swords. The sound grew louder and louder throughout the Pasargadae plane. Cyrus came forward and raised his hand. The sound died when he lowered his hand and addressed the crowd.

"Those who go to battle for their country represent their people."

The warriors cheered. He invited them to silence.

"Today, I am going to make a pledge of allegiance to you and the people under our alliance," he continued, "I pledge myself to establish freedom and justice for all the people under the Persian

Empire."

The cheering and roaring returned to the army. Then he appointed Harpagus as the Medean governor because he was from the same clan as Astiages and therefore would not face an opposition. He arranged the most glorious funeral service for Barzon at the Pasargadae Tower of Silence and buried his bones in a nearby mountain tomb. Astyages and his household were moved to Anshan to live in an allocated palace under watchful eyes of their guards.

With great objectives in mind, Cyrus revolutionized the practice of tribal feudalism and evolved it into a system of central government that was capable of ruling a vast empire formed by different nations of diverse ethnicity and beliefs—a system that maintained its unity and order. Other satraps were under his control while having a local governor with their own rules and regulations. He created one standard interest among different nations to unite them under one command. Democracy, justice, and glory of the empire were his gifts to all nations—a self-sustaining union that could not revolt against itself. He founded the first democratic federal government as he expanded his territory. An intelligent service called the Ears and Eyes of the King, processed general information within the court of local governments, high-ranking authorities, and generals in different fronts. The information would reach a secret council where it was processed further, organized, and brought to his attention.

Chapter 10

Susiana

Following the victory over Astyages, Cyrus decided to organize a campaign and claim Susiana. The Persian ancestors, the Elamites, had built the city and the temple in Susa and founded a great kingdom there. It was part of the Persian territory which had been occupied by Nabonidus of Babylon. The kingdom had to be freed and returned to the Persians. His ears at Susa had informed him that most of Nabonidus' generals were of Medean descent. Now that he had the support of the Medean nation, it was the best time to conquer Susiana.

*****

Araspes arrived at Susa late after midnight. The city gate was closed and he had to wait until morning. Outside the wall, there was a tavern at the riverside among a thicket of oak trees. It provided shelter to those who were left outside the city gate at night. He tied his horse in the stable and went in. The attendant appeared with a goblet of wine and a chalice as soon as he sat down. He felt warm after a few glasses and demanded food. The roasted chicken and warm bread tasted very good for such a tavern. Then, he sat back, observing the few other customers and sipping on his wine.

"I hope you don't mind company."

He looked up at the stranger, clad in merchant's attire.

"I will be grateful if you join me."

The man smiled, revealing overly healthy teeth for his age. *He has been delighted by the compliment,* Araspes thought. The man pulled a chair from the adjoining table and sat opposite Araspes.

"My name is Mihrab, and I trade perfume."

Araspes' deep green eyes regarded the man with respect, trying to guess his origin.

Ancient Susa

"Do not tire your memory, I come from Parthia for business. And you must be coming from Medea?"

"You are right. I was impressed with the good fragrance in the air when I entered the tavern. It must be your perfumes."

"Thank you for the compliment. What brings you to Susa?" Mihrab asked.

"Well, I am a paid warrior. I heard Nabonidus is hiring soldiers. I came to try my luck fighting for him."

"You are indeed lucky. I am going to Abradates' palace tomorrow. His wife, Pantheia, is an admirer of my merchandise."

"His name is familiar—I mean Abradates," Araspes said.

Mihrab lifted his brows, "as a Medean, you must know him well? He is the most powerful general in Nabonidus' army. He is also a Medean, like you are."

He picked up the pitcher of wine just served at their table and filled Araspes' chalice.

"There is something else well-known about Abradates," Mihrab said.

Araspes raised his chalice and sipped the wine. It tasted much better than the one he had been served earlier.

"What else is so well-known about him?" he asked.

"His wife, my friend—Pantheia is indeed the most beautiful woman in Susiana. Her beauty is famous among all."

Araspes widened his eyes and opened his mouth to show surprise.

"You didn't tell me much about yourself. I reckon you are from a noble clan in Medea?" Mihrab asked.

"Well, I am Araspes from Deioces clan—the Medean ruling family for at least one hundred and fifty years," Araspes answered.

"You can ride with me to Abradates' palace tomorrow. I can arrange a meeting," Mihrab said.

*****

The next day, when introduced to Abradates, Araspes requested to speak with him in private. He delivered Cyrus' message, seeking the general's cooperation in freeing Susiana from Babylonian rule. He also informed Abradates of the Persian army's capabilities, emphasizing that Cyrus did not intend to engage in an extensive war and truly meant to avoid bloodshed.

Abradates listened to the message thoughtfully and said that he would dispatch a reliable messenger to Cyrus soon. Then he invited Araspes to join them for dinner. During the feast, Araspes had an opportunity to take a modest look at Pantheia. She was by far more beautiful than he expected. Long black hair decorated her broad, pale shoulders with stunning contrast. Deep sapphire eyes hypnotized the beholder with compassion and wisdom. She was tall, slender and fragile. Her feather-like figure seemed to be gliding in the air as she walked. Her long, green gown brushed the marble floor, awakening its phantoms to watch her hidden beauties. Araspes approached her, doubting whether the goddess-like charm would honor him with a short conversation.

"One moment of exposure to such a beauty is worth all the suffering to reach Susa," he remarked.

She turned, smiled and moved her dress out of the way for more room.

"Thank you. My husband said you are the messenger of the *Shepherd[1]*. I am delighted to hear the promise of freedom and return to the glorious Elamite[2] period," she whispered. "Our nation has had enough of the Babylonian rule."

---

1   A title given to Cyrus by Persians.
2   A n ancient pre-Persian civilization.

Her knowledge during conversation made her beauty even more sensational. Araspes was not surprised by her comment. Mihrab had told him how sophisticated and politically informed she was.

*****

Three months later, Cyrus attacked Susiana. It did not take long for the Persian army to conquer Susa. Abradates had arranged to keep the major part of the Susian army elsewhere on a mission. The people opened the city gates and welcomed the Persian army as soon as they heard that Nabonidus had fled to Babylon.

Officers rode before the foot soldiers and shouted Cyrus' orders. "Do not assault the citizens of Susa. They are your Medean brothers and sisters. Let them feel the joy of freedom."

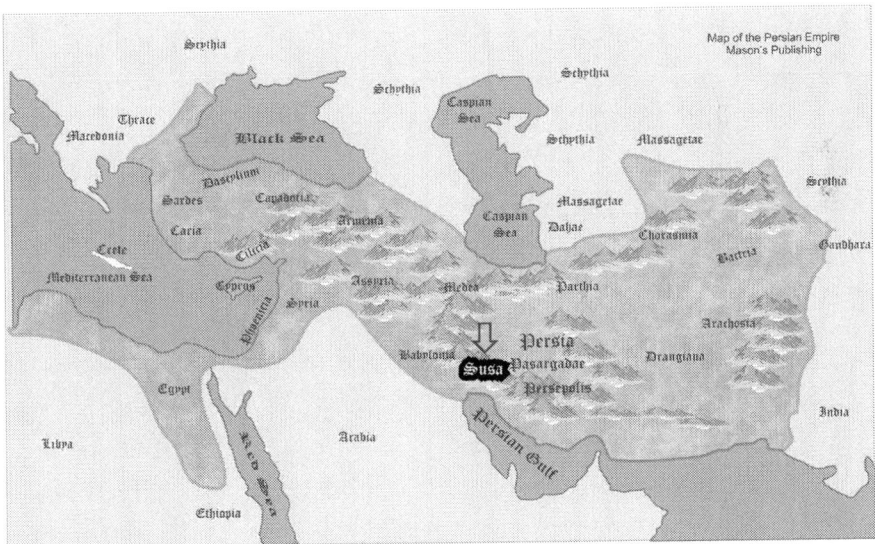

Cult sculptures brought in by Nabonidus from Babylon were scattered all over the city. Regardless of Babylonian belief, they did not possess the power to prevent the Persians from entering the city. There was panic among the people at first. The Persian army, however, had an orderly and friendly behavior. According to Cyrus' direct orders, the soldiers even respected the sculptures, collected them, and kept them in a safe place. Their courteous behavior made the people welcome them as their liberators and embrace them with joy.

Araspes, riding in a leading position before the soldiers, made his way to Abradates' palace. He had orders to protect his household from probable strike. By the time he arrived, the gate had been smashed open. At first, he thought the Persian soldiers had occupied the premises. Inside there was chaos. Slaves were aimlessly running around in the courtyard. This was the first time Araspes encountered Jewish slaves who had been brought from Babylon to Susa by Nabonidus. He stopped one of the slaves. She was a tall, skinny, beautiful girl, wearing a brown robe. Crying fearfully, she held his hand and talked in a language Araspes did not understand. He calmed her down and enquired about Pantheia's whereabouts. Assured that she could trust him, the girl calmed down and gestured that she could lead him to Pantheia. There were a few horses outside the building and Araspes was warned to have a few guards with him for protection.

Inside the palace, the Medean guards were defending the main hall, in which Pantheia was taking refuge. They were outnumbered by Babylonian soldiers, but with the arrival of Araspes and his escorts, the situation changed. The guards, who recognized Araspes from his previous visit, regained their confidence and charged at the Babylonians who retreated and were allowed to escape. The guards cheered and let Araspes inside the main hall. Wearing full armor and holding a long sword, Pantheia blocked the passage to Araspes. He removed his helmet, laughed out loud, and called her by name.

"You look like a goddess in that armor," he said

Pantheia recognized Araspes and relaxed.

"I thought you would never come," she said.

Araspes stood there, looking at her with respect. "I have direct orders from Cyrus to protect your household during the chaos following the siege. I am glad I arrived in time," he said.

Pantheia looked at Marni entering the hall behind Araspes.

"She must have helped you locate me," said Pantheia, pointing at Marni. "She is an intelligent brave girl."

Araspes agreed, pressing the girl's arm warmly. "She volunteered to lead us to your rescue," he said.

Pantheia ran forward and embraced her. "I personally chose to liberate her from a line-up of slave girls in Babylon. She is the daughter of Mathias, a high ranking rabbi who was killed by Babylonians in Jerusalem," she said.

*****

Araspes moved Pantheia and her household to Pasargadae, because they were not safe as long as Abradates was out of Susa. Cyrus had heard of Pantheia's beauty and intelligence from the courtiers but refused to see her. He entrusted her to Araspes until her husband returned. Upon his return, Abradates learned about Cyrus' nobleness from his wife and remained a devoted general in the Persian army all his life.

Araspes married Marni and served as Cyrus' personal guard. Marni would always narrate tales about Jewish slaves in Babylon and how they suffered away from their homeland. Araspes transferred the stories to Cyrus who thought they deserved to be freed from Babylonian captivity. Through Marni, he found contacts among the slaves in Babylon and started collecting strategic information.

Chapter 11

An Inspiring Dream

At this time, Pasargadae was the site of extensive construction. Cyrus had ordered the building of three palaces there. He regarded the region blessed because he had won his first war against Astyages there. Artisans, stone masons, relief makers, wood workers and brick makers had been hired from different parts of the empire. Cyrus had strict laws against slavery throughout the whole confederation. He followed the tradition of his forefathers that people should not be put to work against their will in his kingdom. All workmen and women were paid wages every week.

He personally interviewed the experts and overseers in different fields. He believed unskilled managers in all positions would lead to failure because they would hire amateurish subordinates in order to keep their own authority over the job. Therefore, he hired the most professional experts and laborers to accomplish all the tasks in a perfect manner.

All palaces were surrounded by vast, formal gardens with avenues that stretched before the porches. There were curved limestone basins every ten paces[1] with floral, square, and rectangular designs. On either side of the avenues, there were small streams of running water that irrigated the whole garden.

His private palace, enclosed by porches on either side, was located in the middle of the complex. A flat, round marble stone had been installed at the center of the southeast porch, and conveniently raised from the floor. From there, Cyrus could see a wonderful view of the gardens surrounding the palace.

The gardens were divided into sections to bear Cyrus' four favorite fruits, which he called "fruits of Paradiso": pomegranate, grape, fig and olive. He also ordered that the plains beyond the palaces be cultivated to bear wheat and barley, which he called "food of Paradiso." He also persuaded farmers to raise cattle and sheep, and produce honey, which he called "butter of Paradiso." He emphasized that those nine elements were the source of a healthy and wealthy community.

When in Pasargadae, Cyrus had time to himself and sat there for hours, meditating. Many times before, he had moments of total concentration, when he had deep thoughts about the philosophy of life. During such journeys, he experienced illuminating thoughts about human nature. The more he pondered, the better he perceived man's desires and aspirations and understood how people reacted to different motivations. He then thought of how such reactions could be directed toward their own welfare and happiness. That was the main subject occupying his thoughts on a particular day just before daybreak.

In the immediate view before him, there was a small brook murmuring as it passed around the bend. Occasional falling leaves floated smoothly on the water until caught by some shrub or protruding

1   One pace equals 1.5 meters.

earth in the brook causing slight turbulence. The faint gurgle created by diversion of water from its smooth path had a hypnotic effect. He gradually drifted into a trance.

The dead branches of that giant tree reminded him of his grand-father's dream. He was floating on top of the tree, looking down on a crow watching over an egg in its nest. The egg cracked and a baby vulture hatched. It attacked the crow and started feeding on its corpse. It grew fatter and fatter as it fed. All of a sudden, fresh green sprouts sprang from the dry branches. They grew larger and twisted around the vulture's body, crushing it to pieces as if it had been made of some brittle material. Then the whole tree came alive, as green leaves grew and blossoms appeared all over the branches.

Returning to reality, he heard a heavenly voice proclaiming a message in musical tone. The message was faint and he could not hear it well. He was fully awake, but still trembling from the impact of the vision. The echo of the angelic voice was still vibrating the air around him. Yet, the stench of the decaying vulture filled his nose as if he had carried the foul odor back to the real world. He felt ex-hausted—drops of sweat fell from his forehead. *What an ill-omened vision,* he thought—*except the conclusion*. He felt the warm and soft touch of Cassandane's hands, pressing against his cheeks. She was embracing him tight to stop him from shivering.

"What evil nightmare is troubling my beloved husband?"

Trying to adjust to reality, Cyrus hugged her tight and remained silent for a long time. Twilight penetrated the porch from among the trees. A cool breeze travelling through water fountains touched their skin. Sparrows had started their morning symphony and the whole garden was gradually coming to life.

"Your warm bosom is the sign of a good ending, my love," whispered Cyrus. "I must summon an interpreter. There is an important message to this strange dream."

Later that day, he told Araspes about his dream. Then he summoned an interpreter.

"There is, indeed, a significant message," said the interpreter." Regardless of its apparent decline, the roots of the Persian Empire are going to last for thousands of years because of its principles of justice and fairness. There will be a major invasion of Persian land more than a thousand years from now. It will cause a sinister metamorphosis of culture and belief, imposed on Persians by evil forces. Lies, ignorance, cowardice and cruelty are going to reign for about fourteen hundred years. Before its point of natural destruction, the disciples of this evil cult will take control—an immature practice of power by a dogmatic class. They rise to reveal the dormant ugliness of their obsession and bring corruption to the limit.

Awakened from the long-lasting cultish sleep, a new generation is going to reestablish the Persian values and beliefs again. The corrupted ones are going to be cured and corrected, as their superficial beliefs disappear like powder into the air. Terror and cruelty will vanish as the new generations throughout the world are inspired to reject ignorance. Persia is going to flourish once again and the principles of Human Rights will lead the whole world to prosperity," concluded the interpreter.

Everyone looked at Cyrus for a comment. He thought for few moments and said, "No matter how vicious the invaders and their wicked followers, the goodness will always be victorious at the end."

Chapter 12

The Slaves of Babylon

Nabonidus had taken all precautions to keep the subject of the imminent meeting a secret. Everyone, including the slaves and servants, had been told that a group of merchants were coming from Lydia—an assembly of generals and important members of Lydian high council under the cover of merchants. They arrived in Babylon late, when the city was asleep. They were escorted to the palace straight from the city gate and accommodated in a guesthouse near the palace. Holding a grudge against Cyrus since his defeat in Susiana, Nabonidus was looking forward to this meeting. He was going to convince Croesus to mobilize his army against the Persians. He had already persuaded the Egyptians to support Croesus in this campaign.

He ordered the slaves to go outside as soon as the delegation entered the reception palace. *There must be some important matter to this meeting*, Dara thought while leaving the hall. She knew that the queen's favorite maid, Abby, was now in the secret room observing the event. *I must find an excuse to go there,* she thought. Abby had ordered Dara not to interrupt unless the matter was very important.

Dara was aware of Abby's weaknesses and was planning to create a story when she came across the Garrison Commander peeking around the corner at the maid's private quarters. She knew the maid was having an affair with him. Knowing that Nabonidus was engaged in a lengthy meeting, he had come to see if he could spend some time in private with Abby. That was the opportunity Dara was looking for. She approached the man.

"Is there anything I can help you with, commander?"

Surprised by her voice, the commander turned, "Greetings to you, Dara. I was doing a routine inspection of the guards to make certain everything is at peace in your queen's quarter," he said.

"Is that all you are here for, commander," she said playfully.

"Well, it would not hurt if I could personally report to Abby and see if I could be of service, you know," answered the commander. "Of course, if I could meet her, she would take my word to the queen."

Dara began walking. The commander followed her. "I will take your message to her. I hope it does not disturb her," said Dara.

The commander rubbed his hands. "The security of the royal court is of great importance, you know, especially when a foreign delegation is here," he said, as if pleading with her to take the matter seriously.

Dara told the man to wait for a few minutes while she delivered his message. She knew that Abby would fly back to her quarters to have a nice courtship with him. She then hurried to the secret room with a clever excuse. Upon hearing the message, Abby rushed back to her quarter to meet the commander and Dara was alone in the secret room. She discovered Nabonidus' plans after listening to the ongoing negotiations. Then she decided to meet Laban, the Healer that night.

A few years earlier, Laban had bought himself from slavery, rented a shop in the marketplace, and began trading medicine. He was a loyal member of the Jewish community and secretly supported their struggle for freedom. He had a good reputation among the Babylonian elite. They believed he had a healing touch and great knowledge of herbal medicine. He had a Persian apprentice and managed to learn the language from him. In secret gatherings, he talked of the day when all Jewish slaves in Babylon would be free. He said that the day was near and talked of the Messiah. *I feel his presence*, he would say. He had become very serious about the issue after the fall of Susiana to Persians. He spoke of Cyrus with great respect and believed he was the liberator.

Under the pretext of shopping for some supplies, Dara went out to the marketplace that evening. She made a few stops before meeting Laban. The old man was alone when she entered the shop.

"Dara, I was just thinking about you."

"Here is the opportunity you were looking for," said Dara, putting a piece of folded parchment on the counter top.

"What do you mean, Dara? What opportunity are you talking about?"

"Well, you always said you wished to travel to Persia. This is a very important message for Cyrus and there is no one else I can trust with this mission," said Dara, hurriedly.

"I have been followed and I have to get out of your shop quickly. When you arrive in Anshan, go straight to the palace and find Araspes. He is a Persian general married to my cousin, Marni. Tell him you have a word from me for Cyrus. He will help you deliver the message."

She then reached out and picked up a package of herbal soap from the counter, and headed for the shop door, leaving Laban in confusion.

"Remove the parchment from the counter top immediately," she said, before slamming the door shut.

Laban put the message in a chest and carried on his usual business while discussing the matter with his apprentice, Barman. Their discussion was interrupted once in a while when a shopper entered. He asked Barman to run the shop while he was gone and tell the customers he had gone to import some herbs from India. They closed the shop a little earlier than usual and went to a caravanserai to buy a good horse. The next morning, Laban was on his way to Anshan.

The country road passing through the wheat farms was reminiscent of his childhood in the outskirts of Jerusalem. Breathing the air filled with the scent of fresh wheat and barley was overwhelmingly delightful. The last time Laban experienced this feeling was in the front yard of their farmhouse near Jerusalem. He was playing with the dog, his mother was feeding the chickens, and his father was working in the farm. The wheat had grown to his height and was ready for harvest. The Babylonian soldiers riding on black horses came like demons, bringing their wrath upon his family. The chickens ran as if chased by foxes. He still remembered the man who pushed his mother inside the house. Laban tried to hold him by the leg, but was kicked away, and the Babylonian uttered a curse he did not understand. A brief look at the man's face registered everything in his childish mind—a thick mustache, scar on his lower cheek, and six fingers on his left hand—strangely funny in that terrible situation. They raped his mother while his father, tied to a tree, was crying with agony. Then the same man killed his father in cold blood. They carried him away to Babylon. He never found out about the fate of his mother.

*****

Croesus was a cunning leader. He came up with artful plots and tactics during battles and prepared different fail-safe plans so that he could switch from one to another in case of a failure. He knew that Cyrus would have all the information about his army before he reached the Persian borders. He planned to prepare a small army, consisting of about one hundred thousand men, with light weapons and armor. He did not intend to include heavily armored vehicles and wagons. That way, his army could move very fast and he would have an opportunity to draw Cyrus into his trap. A guard announced the entrance of a visitor. Croesus was looking forward to this meeting. The visitor was Artacamas, his own nephew and Cyrus' cousin.

Artacamas bowed to his uncle, Croesus, and remained that way until spoken to. The emperor moved forward and patted his shoulder.

"The time has come for the opportunity we were looking for," Croesus said. "Now, you can help re-instate your grandfather to the Medean throne and achieve your longtime objective, the sovereignty of Susiana."

Artacamas looked happy. "I have heard of your preparation to attack Persia. It will be an honor for me to fight in your army."

Croesus grinned. "I have a more important mission for you—an extremely secret mission. I want you to proceed to Persia and meet Cyrus."

Artacamas frowned. "What would be the purpose of this meeting?" he enquired.

"Well..." Croesus walked to the table beside his throne. There was a small box on the table. He opened the box and produced a small pouch. He held the pouch, dangling from a delicate silk thread. Artacamas was confused.

"This is the key to our success. It contains a very strong poison. It had an instantaneous effect on Barzon during the battle of Pasargadae. Just a scratch will do the job. Think of the consequences."

Artacamas nodded in understanding. "Approaching Cyrus directly would definitely raise suspicion. I will not be able to get closer than the reception palace."

"That is very clever of you. I know I am not mistaken in choosing you for this mission," said Croesus. "The meeting must be totally accidental. You can start by requesting to visit your grandfather, Astyages, and your Aunt, Aryenis—or just think of something."

*****

Laban was traveling along the Persian Royal Road. He had heard there were caravansaries[1] every ten to fifteen parasang[2]. It was early evening when he saw lights in the distance. As he got closer, the smell of fresh bread awakened his appetite. He was checked and interrogated by the guards to verify he was a traveler, and not an agent of the bandits, before being permitted into the castle.

The interior of the structure was much more complicated than its simple exterior walls. It had been built in two sections. The inner section included small rooms with a front porch overlooking the pond in the center of the courtyard. Behind the rooms there were

1   Fortified out-of-town inns for caravans and travelers to stay overnight.

2   Ancient Persian measure of distance approximately equal to six kilometers. League, the distance a horse could walk in one hour.

stables with access doors opening into the passageway, leading to the entrance gate and other occasional openings in-between the rooms. There was a tavern at one corner where Laban ate, and then he went to bed early. The next morning before leaving, he met Artacamas for the first time as he was preparing his horse to leave.

An ancient caravanserai

"Dorood[1]!" Artacamas said, speaking in Persian tongue.

Laban was delighted to hear someone talk to him in the language he had learned from his apprentice. Now he could practically use his skills.

"Dorood!" He answered.

"I saw you entering the caravanserai last night. You must be heading east, I guess," Artacamas said.

"Well, I am heading for Anshan," Laban answered.

"Great, I hope you don't mind company," Artacamas said. "I am heading in the same direction."

"I will be happy to have company on this long journey," Laban said, regarding Artacamas with caution. *I should be careful. He must not suspect the true purpose of my travel.*

1   Persian word for "Greetings." Hello.

Laban told the man that he was on a business trip to buy herbs from Persia and possibly India. Artacamas tried to gain his trust. He found out that Laban had influential friends in Anshan. He told Laban that he intended to register in the Persian army and serve Cyrus.

Upon arrival they stayed in a town caravanserai near the palace. Laban was very excited to meet King Cyrus in person. He had heard about his conquest of Susiana and liberation of the slaves. In Babylon, the people called him the Liberator. Even the Babylonian generals respected him as a just conqueror.

At the Gate-House Palace, Laban was guided to a bench in the main hall to wait until he was given further notice. The hall had eight stone columns about fifty trayas[1] high. The architecture was magnificent and pleasing to the eye. Immediately after entering the hall, the opposite wall attracted his attention. It was decorated with a stone relief of a winged creature wearing a crown with two horns and three fishlike conical figures. It reminded him of an Egyptian mythological character, seeking the water of life in an imaginary mountain. He was wearing an Elamite[2] costume. On top of the relief there was a simple inscription in Persian, Babylonian, and another language he did not recognize. It read: "I am Cyrus, the Achaemenian King."

The wings showed that the figure was hovering over the ground as if flying. Laban remembered the prophecies of Isaiah[3] one hundred and forty years before their temple was demolished by Babylonians:

1   Ancient Persian unit of length equal to 300 millimeters, which is about one foot.

2   Ancient civilization in Mesopotamia about 2700-1100 BC.

3   Prophet of ancient Israel after whom the biblical book of Isaiah is named. Isaiah's call to prophecy came c. 742 BC.

"...Who roused from the east him that victory hails at every step? Who presents him with nations, subdues kings to him? His sword makes dust of them and his bow scatters them like straw. He pursues them and advances unhindered, his feet scarcely touching the road. Who is the author of this deed if not he who calls the generations from the beginning? I, the Lord, who am the first and shall be with the last." (Isaiah 41:2-4)

And then, he explicitly explains the alliance between Cyrus and God: "Thus says the Lord to his anointed, to Cyrus, whom he has taken by his right hand to subdue nations before him and strip the loins of kings, to force gateways before him that their gates be closed no more: I will go before you levelling the heights. I will shatter the bronze gateways, smash the iron bars. I will give you the hidden treasures, the secret hoards, that you may know that I am the Lord." (Isaiah 45:1-3)

"We can go now," Araspes said, breaking his concentration.

From the hall, they entered a very pleasant garden and followed a lush, winding avenue, leading to the reception palace. They crossed a porch with many columns and arrived at the entrance gate. There were huge slabs of dark limestone on either side, decorated with the relief of a celestial creature with eagle claws guarding the palace. The guards came to attention as they saw Araspes.

They entered a very spacious hall with high pillars, the base of which had carvings of lotus flowers. He had heard that it was the symbol of water in Persian Zoroastrian philosophy. The other symbol was fire represented by a lion. Laban looked up and found the same inscription as in the Gate House Palace in three languages on top of the pillars. The words were very straightforward and indicated the practical and direct personality of Cyrus. At the opposite end of the hall, he saw King Cyrus on his throne with courtiers around him.

His heart started pounding heavily as they approached. Finally, he found himself face to face with Cyrus. *Oh, Great God, what a modest man he is!*

He was a man in his thirties, wearing an Elamite costume. His oval face, pointed nose, and short black beard blended with a charismatic smile. He was of medium height, wore a light crenelated crown and a short sword. There was no sign of jewelry on him, except for a simple silver necklace.

"Come near, Laban," said Cyrus. "I heard you carry a message from our dear friend, Dara."

Laban was excited. Cyrus had called him by name.

"May Jehovah bless you and make his face shine toward you," Laban said, kneeling and stretching out his hand, holding the parchment.

"I am honored, my lord," he added.

On his way back to the carvanserai, Laban thought about his conversation with Cyrus, realizing he was way ahead of his time—*more of a philosopher than a warrior*, he thought. When Laban brought up the subject of religion, he had remarked, "It is not the religion I respect, but the people who follow genuine values no matter what their faith." Cyrus was a Zoroastrian himself, nevertheless, he respected the right of all his citizens to practice the religion of their choice.

*****

Cyrus had a long-term strategy to conquer Lydia, but changed his approach when he learned Croesus had already organized his army to attack Persia. He knew that Croesus' motives were to prevent the Persian invasion of Lydia while trying to re-instate his brother-in-law, Astyages, to the Medean throne. Cyrus had previously sent delegations to advise Egyptians, Chaldeans, and Spartans to avoid joining Croesus. His *ears* had informed him of the number of men in the Lydian army. He decided to mobilize his military and camp near the Halys River at the border of the Persian Empire. There he could attack and follow the Lydians with fresh forces before they had a chance to revive themselves after the long march across Lydia. It was late autumn when his army began the march.

Chapter 13

The Battle of Pteria

A cold wind blowing across the dead riverbed behind them carried the stench of the decaying fish. The chill in the air numbed their fingers. Their eyes were red from the long, sleepless nights invading Cappadocia. Their shields felt heavier and their grip was loose. It had been a long time since they ate a decent meal—hot food, fresh bread, and a deep sleep were mere memories. On the horizon, the Persians were marching in great numbers with incredible discipline. The pounding on their shields had a crushing effect. The sound came from all directions. Thump! Thump! Thump! A few beats of silence, and then again. Thump! Thump! Thump! The chariots riding along the orderly blocks of foot soldiers glittered in the distance.

Preceding his campaign, Croesus had sent a gold statue, some jewelry, and other gifts to the Oracle of Delphi, seeking her advice to predict if it were safe for him to attack Persia. The Oracle had vaguely advised:

"If Croesus mobilizes an army against the Persians and crosses the Halys River, a powerful empire will be terminated." Croesus was delighted by the prediction. He simply interpreted the comment to his benefit and organized an army to attack Persia.

After a long march across Lydia, the army camped at the Halys riverbank, preparing for a tough quest. The task of crossing the river was entrusted to Thales[1], the philosopher and engineer. He inspected the riverbank and found an area where the land was low and flat, and instructed the army to camp there as compactly as possible. Afterwards, he had the laborers dig a canal behind the army in the shape of a crescent and diverted the river. The riverbed in front of the army became dry, and they passed.

At last, Croesus had crossed the river, and set foot on the northwestern borders of Cappadocia, which had been attached to the Persian Empire after the conquest of Medea—a highland limited to Armenia in the east, the Euxine Sea in the north, and Euphrates River in the south. Now, he would sack their cities, intimidating the people in other satrapies to prevent the formation of a solid resistance against his army. Croesus thought of that as a great conquest; however, he was disappointed as he entered the cities. The Cappadocians had prepared themselves long before the arrival of his army—a wise and timely tactic originated by Cyrus to demoralize the Lydian forces after their first conquest. The hungry and exhausted soldiers entered the deserted cities. Everything of value including cattle, sheep, and crops had been moved to caves and camps in the mountains. The promise of the tender lambs from the highland pastures of Cappadocia was only a mirage. They had to make do with the tough boiled barley and salted whale meat brought from the Euxine Sea. Invading Cappadocia, after all, was an insignificant conquest and a waste of energy.

The Persians had camped in strategic positions. They would at-

1   Greek philosopher, mathematician, and astronomer.

tack at night with small groups of archers who fired deadly arrows with precision. When followed, they still shot fatal arrows at their pursuers while galloping away and disappearing into the wooded areas. The Lydian lancers were no match for them. Tired of such attacks, they were trapped in their camps, until Croesus decided to confront Cyrus in the open field. As he marched his army out of the city, taking up a position east of the Halys River, the Persians abruptly appeared in the plain where he planned to camp. He finally found himself facing Cyrus, whom the Persians called "The Shepherd"—a man who guides his people to prosperity. Croesus had taken that with a grain of salt.

Cyrus had planned to confront Croesus at a rough terrain where it was hard for the cavalry and chariots to maneuver. Thus, he would gain advantage because his infantrymen, including archers and slingers, had been specifically trained to engage in face to face combat, demanding swordsmanship and physical aggression. He watched and commanded the war from the top of a hill overlooking the battleground. The Lydian infantry forces were crossing the terrain before the cavalry when Cyrus motioned Harpagus to attack. The Lydians stopped in their positions as the Persians approached the firing range. The first wave of arrows from the Lydian side blackened the sky, and the Persians formed a wall of shields in front and overhead. Then they retaliated with an effective overhead fire, targeting the line of forces behind the Lydian infantry who were at a disadvantage because of the rough terrain. The stacked corpses and natural barrier restricted the chariots and the cavalry who were trying to support the isolated infantry. As the Lydians showed confusion, the Persians charged—fast and fierce. The battle continued for many hours and countless soldiers died from both sides.

The sun grew bigger and turned red, smearing the gathering clouds with blood from the horizon. A nipping whisper of wind signaled the approaching storm. The warriors started retiring to their camps and the chaos came to a sudden stop. The battleground was covered with many corpses and wounded soldiers. Darkness gradually prevailed. The storm and heavy snow spread a white sheet on the dead in the battleground. The wailing and begging of the injured continued all night. The lanterns shone like glowworms while the soldiers from both sides searched and carried the wounded to their camp.

The freezing wind continued and the Persians, being at an advantage, held their positions. Many days passed quietly on both fronts, and neither of the forces showed any tendency to engage in combat. Winter storms confined the Lydians in their camp. Croesus' informants, including Artacamas, had sent news that the Persians outnumbered the Lydians two to one. His generals reminded him that the failure in Cappadocia and the freezing weather had reduced the morale of their units. The region would be snowbound for another two months, and Cyrus was not making any move to further the war. Therefore, it would be a wise decision to withdraw to Sardis, and wait for the summer. He sent word to his allies in Egypt, Babylon, and Ionia to gather their forces and be prepared within five months. Besides, his envoys were now organizing fresh units in Sardis. He would withdraw, organize all these forces, and march against the Persians again. He ordered his generals to commence the retreating operation.

*****

"Let him withdraw," Harpagus advised Cyrus. "We will be on his tail. Most of his allies will avoid him when they find out that he is on the run. Besides, we will be between him, the Babylonians, and the Assyrians."

"He will have the advantage of the mounted troops, and the choice of battleground in the next engagement. We must come up with a plan to disable his cavalry and chariots before further confrontation," said Cyrus.

From far away, came the neighing of horses. Harpagus went out of the tent and looked down the hill. The soldiers were moving some Lydian chargers to the stables behind the front lines. Cyrus joined him outside the tent.

"I made an interesting discovery today," Harpagus said, looking down the hill. "the Lydian chargers are sensitive to the smell of our beasts of burden."

"Do you mean the camels?" asked Cyrus.

"Yes, my lord," Harpagus pointed at a few horses creating disorder among the troops. "Unlike our Nisayan chargers, they run in a frenzy at the sight of the camels."

"Interesting," said Cyrus, following the direction of the chargers galloping across the camp.

"That piece of information alone could win us a war, my lord" Harpagus said with a smile.

"Bright idea. We can put their cavalry out of commission by running a herd of camels in front of our lines," Cyrus said, patting Harpagus on the shoulder. "Let's send for more herds from Assyria."

Before the nightfall, the clouds disappeared. A clear, starry sky and full moon helped Croesus move his army across the river.

Chapter 14

The Battle of Thymbra

Cyrus ordered Harpagus to call for an assembly of his generals. He wanted to talk to them before they got drunk celebrating their victory over the Lydians. The Armenian and Cappadocian commanders argued that the enemy had been defeated, and the snowbound plateau was too harsh an environment to render a plentiful harvest. Their troops wished to spend the cold winter in the peace and security of their villages, helping their families with fishing and hunting to pass the winter. Some Medeans also yearned for the warm climate of Ekbatana. The commanders from seven Persian tribes did not make any comment and waited for Cyrus to speak.

Apart from 85,000 Persian and Hyrcanian warriors, the major part of his army was composed of the Medes, the Armenians, and the Cappadocians. Almost all generals expressed the feeling that they must rest in their homes for the winter and gather again in summertime.

After listening to everyone's advice, Cyrus said, "My good allies, I am not acting as a triumphant warrior greedy for a second victory. This is not a matter of defense or winning a battle. We have the best opportunity to overthrow the Lydian Empire at this time. If we retreat to the comfort of our homes now, it would be a very difficult task to defeat Croesus in the summer. He will have his allies by his side and will fight with a higher morale. His forces will be fresh, well-fed, and combat-ready. His troopers will be organized. He will take advantage of the rich harvest along his way to our lands, and will not have to carry a heavy train of provisions."

Cyrus paused for a moment to assess the impact of his speech. He had many friends among the Medean generals. He was hoping for their cooperation. He particularly looked at Raspas, an influential general among the Medes, and knew he could count on him to passionately recruit among the Medean troopers. He also had close ties with Tigranes, the Armenian commander. A long time ago, Cyrus had gone on a hunting trip to Armenia with his grandfather and made friends with him. He was sure neither would fail him.

"But, if we follow the Lydians now," he continued, "we will rest in Sardis after defeating Croesus. We should not waste the opportunity while we have the upper hand. We will follow and surprise him. By the time we arrive at Sardis, it will be early spring and we will have a good rest after putting an end to his rule. All our forces will have a chance to share the riches of the Lydian Empire."

The generals looked at each other in agreement and rested their fists on their hearts in solidarity. Cyrus mobilized his army westward across Lydia toward the warmer climate—through the valleys covered with olive gardens and rich lands where sheep and cattle grazed in the natural pastures that provided food for the Persian Nisayan Chargers.

Croesus arrived at Sardis in late winter. He knew he could not enjoy resting in the comfort of his palace for long. While retreating to his capital, he had been informed that Cyrus was on his tail with an army of 200,000 men. He sent word to his allies to accelerate their campaign. This time, he could outnumber the enemy two to one. His allies were arriving in Sardis by the thousands—120,000 Egyptians, 60,000 Babylonians, and about 220,000 Lydians and Hellespont nations. In the valley of Thymbra, Croesus spread his army in an area of five miles. They were more organized than in the Battle of Pteria. Egyptians, however, had their own independent formation and were drawn up in blocks of ten-thousand. Croesus had positioned his menacing cavalry in the front. They were backed by chariots, countless infantries, and archers. He was confident his powerful horsemen would gain advantage over the enemy at an early stage.

While Croesus was busy arranging his forces across the valley, Cyrus called a meeting of his generals and officers. They informed him of the rumors about the enemy's growing strength, regardless of all the efforts to engage the soldiers in sport and other activities in order to keep them from gossip. The rumors, however, circulated fast and caused lowering morale among the Persian soldiers. Cyrus knew that if he tried to revive the army's high spirit, the enemy agents would make it ineffective. The day before the final confrontation, he ordered all generals to prepare the forces for battle very early in the morning. As the sun was rising in the east, the Persian army was ready to march. It was time to deliver his well-prepared speech. Total silence dominated as he addressed the army. His strong voice echoed across the valley.

"My supporters and allies. We have been fighting to defend a good cause—the one and only right worth dying for—freedom!" He paused, while officers and interpreters transferred his message far across the encampment.

The army cheered. He knew that his agents would carry the

highlights of his speech to the enemy lines.

"We extend this virtuous cause even to our enemies, their subjects, and slaves. We want freedom for everyone."

He paused again and waited for the shouting and hailing to subside.

"This is the enemy we have defeated before. Now they have hired mercenaries to fight for them. Most of them have been shipped here against their will. They know our fearless army has all the ingredients necessary to defeat them—gallant cavalry, chariots equipped with offensive weapons, horses shielded by armors, and towers on wheels to fire thousands of deadly arrows at them."

The voices of interpreters in different divisions and the cries of approval from the crowd were promising. He had accomplished his purpose. Confidence and courage were returning to his warriors.

"We have word from our friends that most of the enemy forces think of us as a liberating army, and they are psychologically ready to join us. Let's prove to them that we are indeed invincible, and they have no choice other than submission. We shall defeat this enemy again."

The whole army started clanging their swords on their shields, trying to demoralize the enemy before engaging in physical combat. His speech was over. The warriors were ready for battle. He turned and faced the Lydian troops. Everybody could see him on the hill. He raised both hands, holding short swords, and aimed at the enemy lines with his right hand while holding the left upward. That was the sign to wait for the opponent to attack first.

As the Lydian troopers charged, a line of camels came rushing forward from behind the formations and through the large spaces between them. They formed a charging force in the front line. They waited for the Lydian cavalry to reach the firing range. Then the camels started moving toward them. At the sight of the huge animals, the Lydian chargers became crazed. The confusion brought their cavalry to a sudden stop.

Then the Persian archers started firing at them. The deadly arrows hit man and animal, bringing chaos to the Lydian forces. At that point, the Persian cavalry attacked, riding around the dismounted Lydian lancers who were no match for the Persian horsemen firing swift arrows. The Lydian cavalry was thus put out of commission and the Persian archers shifted to new positions, firing at the infantry. By the end of the day, the scattered Lydians admitted defeat and took refuge within the high walls of the city, closing the gates behind them.

The Persian forces followed the enemy to the city gates, and then camped in the rich valleys around the city, seeking forage and provisions. The following day, Cyrus arranged a grand funeral for Abradates who had been killed in the battle of Thymbra. They buried him at the bank of the peaceful Pactolus[1] River. His wife, Pantheia, appeared at the grave side. Her red-rimmed eyes and distant look revealed an intense sorrow for losing her husband. She acted strangely absent when spoken to. Following the burial, she demanded to be alone at her husband's grave. After a few minutes, they found her dead on the grave stone. She had committed suicide. They buried her by her husband. Cyrus ordered a monument to be raised in their memory for the courage they had shown serving their country.

*****

The abandoned farmers outside the city walls were terrified, for

---

1   A river near the Aegean coast of Turkey.

they thought the victorious warriors would sack their villages and take them into slavery. But the victors did not lay a hand on the people, nor did they try to loot their farms and villages. They were kind and merciful to the people, and soon everything returned to normal. Farmers went to their farms and other people to their businesses. In some cases, even the Persian soldiers helped farmers in their work. They pitched their tents and stayed in their camps, performing their usual routine of practicing with bow and arrow, riding horses, and other training activities.

Chapter 15

The Siege of Sardis

Before sundown, Croesus went out to the courtyard behind the citadel. The wind whispering in his ear carried the pleasant cool air of approaching spring. The boundless valley, far below his feet, was covered with thousands of the Persian army tents. To his surprise, the towns and villages were peaceful, untouched, and no sacking or looting was in progress. There was no sign of bloodshed or groups of captives roped together to be taken to slave markets. Everything was calm, and the Persian troops were going about their routine business as if they were camping in their own hometown. As the sun disappeared in the waters of the west, lanterns were lighted in the camp. It was a spectacular scene—a panorama of lights stretching long distances disappearing in the horizon.

The chilly night wind broke his daze. He pulled up his cloak to cover his ears. *Any man with such an attitude can win the heart of his subjects.* He admired Cyrus for such a civilized behavior towards a defeated enemy, and regretted his own conduct with the remaining people in the city when he occupied Cappadocia. Looking back at the Persian encampment, he thought, *How could one train so many people to control their manners when they defeated an enemy?* The valley was sinking into silence now. He could hear the sound of a distant harp accompanied by a Persian song.

I am free to roam,
the sky and land at will.
To drift as a twig,
on currents with thrill.

Heaven is yonder,
people wander free.
Liberty to ponder,
bellow the olive tree.

Having felt the nearness of the final defeat, Croesus arranged a ritual in his private temple. He still believed that the Goddess, Artemis, was invincible and extended her qualities to true worshipers. Some voice inside him, however, insisted that he must be prepared for unfavorable events. He gathered all his wives and trusted eunuchs during the ritual, and announced that he would offer his body in sacrifice to the Gods if the Persians succeeded in breaking

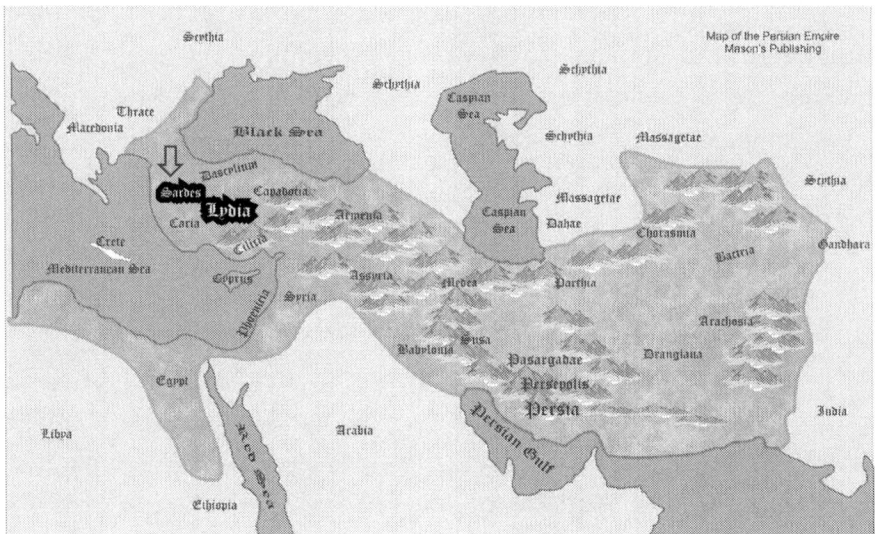

into Sardis. He ordered the eunuchs to shed the blood of his wives and sacrifice them to Goddess Artemis, once he threw himself into the already prepared pyre in the courtyard of the palace.

*****

All attempts to penetrate the city walls had failed. Cyrus asked his generals to come up with a solution to open the city gates. Hyroiades was a Mardian highlander who served in the cavalry division of the Persian army. He was among the group who were sent on a mission to locate penetrable spots in the city fortification. The previous night, on his first round, he noticed that the citadel lodging the palace was built on a high cliff, seemingly impenetrable from the outside. This night, he was going to inspect the stronghold more closely.

The full moon poured a bright blue light on the cliff. The cold wind pierced his body and made him restless. He sat there, under a tree, for a few hours, watching the activities on top of the cliff. Apparently, the guards did not pay much attention to that side of the citadel. The only guard on watch kept away from the edges. *The wind must be blowing hard at that height,* he thought. A moment later, the guard's helmet was snatched by the wind and bounced off the stony slopes to rest at a bush near the foot of the cliff. Hyroiades became more curious as the guard climbed down through some winding path with amazing agility to recover his helmet. He memorized the path, tried it once, and then informed General Harpagus of his findings. The same night, a group of highlanders, Medes, and Persians, with Hyroiades in the lead, climbed the cliff and opened the gates. The Persian army stormed the city of Sardis.

The guards informed Croesus that the palace was under attack by the Persians. He went to the courtyard immediately and ordered the pyre be ignited. Then he sent his eunuchs to do away with his wives who were praying in the temple. He approached the blazing fire, but the heat and fear of death prevented him from jumping into the fire. He looked at the men about him. They were intently waiting to see what he would do next. None of the faces looked familiar. He enquired about his officers. They spoke in a strange tongue he did not understand. He realized they were the Persian warriors who had already taken control of the palace. They did not harm him or force him to do anything against his will, but a few of them always accompanied him wherever he went. They had also rescued his wives from the deadly daggers of his eunuchs. Following Cyrus' orders of giving priority to negotiation over mere force, General Harpagus convinced Croesus to command his army to surrender.

The following day, the Persian army officially entered the city. Croesus, wearing ceremonial garments, appeared at the gate of his palace and welcomed the victorious generals, pleading with them not to burn the palace.

"We shall not burn what belongs to us," Harpagus told him.

Croesus proudly gave a tour of his palace to his captors, showing his artwork collection of statues and paintings. Finally, he called in the treasurer and led the delegation through a labyrinth of passages to the crypt containing the riches of the Lydian Empire. Harpagus, the Persian army commander, said something to him that made everyone laugh. The interpreter by his side translated, "We would like to relieve you of all these burdens. You are going to have a worry-free sleep tonight." Deep inside, Croesus thought that the man was right, and he felt as if he had been relieved of all his concerns.

Cyrus ordered his generals to encamp in the city and keep their men at their posts. He also demanded that all renegade attempts to pillage the city be controlled. Then he ordered Croesus be brought to his presence.

"Hail, King Cyrus, my lord and master! So I salute you, for the gods themselves have given you that title."[1]

The confident behavior of Croesus surprised Cyrus. He stood up and greeted the defeated emperor.

"Hail to you, likewise," answered Cyrus, "for we are both men, and neither of us is a god. Tell me now: would you be willing to advise me as a friend?"[2]

"Gladly—and more than gladly," said Croesus. "I will help you all I can."

Then Cyrus talked to Croesus in private, seeking his advice.

"Wise emperor of Lydia, you have had sovereignty over many nations. Enlightened men such as Thales and Solon[3] have served in your court. Therefore, you are the best advisor to direct me on what to do at this time."

"What troubles you, my lord?" Croesus asked.

"My warriors have been away from home for a long time, and now they have conquered the richest city in the region. They naturally expect their reward. We do not have much time. Soon, the villains among my forces are going to start whispering antagonism among the soldiers and hoist the banner of rebellion. To prevent such a revolt, I will have to allow Sardis to be plundered against my will. Therefore, I am seeking your advice to help me think of a remedy," Cyrus answered.

1 Xenophon's Cyrus the Great: The arts of leadership and war.

2 Xenophon's Cyrus the Great: The arts of leadership and war.

3 An Athenian statesman, lawmaker, and poet.

Croesus had already grown fond of this noble man. He was impressed by Cyrus' honorable behavior and also regarded him as the healer of his son.

"My lord, earlier when your soldiers stormed my palace, I was trying to protect my son who has been deaf and dumb all his life. One of your warriors tried to spear me out of his way when my son called out to him, 'Do not harm him—he is Croesus, my father.' That was a miracle to me and, in my heart, I regarded you as a healer who granted my wish to hear my son speak. Now, I am ready to help you with all my heart."

"The people of Sardis are very wealthy. I will send word to them that I have made a pact with you not to sack the city, and their families will be given security from slavery. In return, I will ask them to bring you the riches of Sardis. You can distribute these treasures among your warriors. This way, everyone will get a share, and you will win the favor of your men even more."

"Perfect," Cyrus said, "I knew you would think of a wise solution."

As the defeated emperor was leaving, Cyrus thought, *the old fox will still need watching.* He would have to take Croesus and his family with him when leaving Sardis. Tabalus, one of the Persian military commanders, and Pactyes the Lydian, were appointed as the first satrap[1] of Sardis and its treasurer, respectively. Then Cyrus set out from Sardis to return to Persia. Croesus distributed and loaded some of the treasures of his empire, and riches collected from the people of Sardis into a caravan of wagons. Before departing for Sardis, Cyrus summoned the commanders of all divisions and instructed them to divide the contents of the wagons among their subordinates. He told Croesus that the treasures would be protected

1   Governor.

better that way, because they belonged to the soldiers now and he would not have to worry about safeguarding them. Croesus was indeed impressed with his wisdom.

Following the conquest of Sardis, Cyrus returned to Pasargadae and spent a few years there while his generals were busy expanding his empire in the east. He also expanded his cavalry to forty thousand horsemen. Chrysantas, the Medean, served as the commander of the cavalry division. He had joined the Persian army during the Battle of Pteria, and stayed very close to Cyrus since. During those years, Cyrus was in touch with Dara who sent the news from Nabonidus ' court. Croesus had told Cyrus that the idea of invading Persia was first suggested by Nabonidus. This information confirmed Dara's warning delivered by Laban. Cyrus had, now, enough reasons to organize a campaign against Nabonidus. He decided to arrange an expedition into the city of Babylon before mobilizing his army. The only person he could trust to carry his message to Dara, was Laban. After meeting with Cyrus, Laban had been working as a dispenser in one of the infirmaries in the army. Later, he was promoted as the headmaster of the mobile hospital in the cavalry division under the supervision of Chrysantas. As an apprentice, Artacamas had kept close to Laban, looking for an opportunity to accomplish the mission set by his uncle, Croesus. After the fall of Sardis, he lost faith in Croesus and thought to get close to Nabonidus. Now that Laban was on a mission to Babylon, it was the best opportunity to go with him, meet Nabonidus, and express his devotion to him. He was not aware of the reason Laban was going to Babylon, but he thought he could make him speak throughout the trip.

*****

Riding along with Laban reminded Artacamas of the start of their friendship when they were travelling to Persia. His motives had not changed and he was still thinking of revenge. He was determined to hurt Cyrus' interest in any way he could. Now that Croesus had been overthrown, his original mission was canceled, and now he was seeking a new sponsor to continue his plot. They stayed at a caravansary at night, and while drinking some wine and eating kebab, Artacamas found out that Laban had a message for Dara, a slave woman who worked in the private quarters of Nabonidus. At breakfast, Artacamas poisoned Laban's drink, left him in agony, and fled the lodge. When arrived at Babylon, he met Nabonidus, introduced himself, and told him of Cyrus' intention to attack Babylon. Dara, who was listening to their conversation from the secret chamber, sent a messenger to inform their allies of Artacamas' betrayal and the proximity of danger. Later that day, she was arrested in her quarters while preparing to escape.

Chapter 16

An Expedition

Following the fall of Sardis, Nabonidus started strengthening his defenses. He had allied with Croesus by sending 20,000 warriors to help the campaign against Cyrus. He had also occupied Susiana and enslaved many Persians earlier. There were more than 40,000 Jewish slaves in Babylon and Cyrus planned to liberate them. He knew Cyrus would attack Babylonia soon. The city had been built as a strategic stronghold with high impenetrable walls. General Harpagus had already prepared a good report with sketches to show the fortifications from all sides. Cyrus had reviewed it briefly. Laban had also told him a lot about Babylon because he had lived there since childhood. Regardless of all his information, Cyrus decided to organize an expedition into the city of Babel to evaluate vulnerability of their defenses before planning an assault against Nabonidus.

Outside the walls, the Hebrew workers whispered to each other, "Roused from the east, him that victory hails at every step, the Mashiach[1] will shatter the bronze gateways, smash the iron bars." Money changers spread the rumor, and the transcriber of words in

1   Messiah.

the temple interpreted the expression as referring to Cyrus whose army was camping far away in the plains and pastures north of Babylon. Nabonidus believed Cyrus presented no threat to Babylon. He thought the fortified walls would not be passable for his army.

The news from Sardis and rumors of imminent war had raised the price of food, especially wheat and sugar. The temple destiny-seers said Bel-Marduk1 was angry. They demanded more gold and slaves in order to arrange a major procession for public prayer and worship. *I can hold the hands of Marduk in public to prove my devotion to the great God of Babylon*, Nabonidus contemplated. The ceremony would also strengthen his position against his son, Belshazzar, who was waiting for an opportunity to unseat him. It was a foolish move to face Cyrus in the open plains, yet Belshazzar was possessed by the temptation and was preparing for the campaign. Nabonidus would do nothing against his son and let Cyrus teach him a lesson. Then he would reinforce his authority, become the heroic defender of Babylon, and secretly punish the gang of priests who had turned away from him. Belshazzar had won the favor of the soldiers by organizing a great feast with abundant food and wine for the army on New Year's Eve, and soon would pose a danger to his throne. He would deal with the threat when his son returned as a defeated commander. It was the month of Nisan and barley was ripe for harvest. The Persian army had already collected their share of the yield in the territories north of Babylon.

*****

"Unbelievable!" said Cyrus. "I could not have imagined its immensity until I saw it. How thick is it?" he asked, looking at Chrysantas.

---

1   Babylonian God.

"My lord, many people believe it is fifty royal cubits[1] in thickness," Chrysantas answered. "Besides, the bulk of it is made of baked brick, a mixture of cement and bitumen[2] as mortar, and reed as shock absorber," he added.

Cyrus' eyes widened. "It is impenetrable. As I can see, we cannot climb it either—looks very high."

"It is two hundred cubits in height," Harpagus remarked.

"People exaggerate about things, yet I have seen with my own eyes," Chrysantas interrupted. "There is a road up there on top of that wall, stretching all around the city. You can easily drive a four-horse chariot on that road."

Ancient Babylon

---

1   One cubit is equal to 1.64 feet.

2   Asphalt made from cement and mortar in ancient times.

"The sides seem to be almost four parasangs[1]," Cyrus said. "It takes an enormous amount of manpower and many years of hard work to build such a fortification."

"Jewish slaves suffered for many years to build it—they worked their fingers to the bone here," Harpagus said .

The boatman warned them to hold fast, for they were approaching the dock. Ishtar Gate was the most crowded of the eight gates around the city of Babylon. The magnificent structure was made of glazed brick with different shades of olive and gold. It was about thirty cubits high and sixty cubits wide. The lintel, walls, and the two towers on either side, were decorated with golden reliefs of dragons, lions, and bulls framed in stripes bearing lotus flowers. The canal was loaded with boats—Hebrew money changers, bankers of exchange, procurers, guesthouse solicitors, peddlers, and beggars along the canal bank.

"You don't need to dock, we are not disembarking," said Chrysantas, in the Assyrian tongue.

The boatman looked at them with suspicion. They had presented themselves as horse traders and experience told him they possessed heavy pouches of gold coins under their garments. "This is the end of your trip across the canal, mister. It's getting dark and no longer safe to stay on the water."

Cyrus winked at Chrysantas and said, "We will disembark right here, good man."

The sun hid behind the high walls and darkness fell all of a sudden. A money-changer boat approached them. One of the crew members repeated a phrase in different languages. "Master, we give you the best shekel for your money." Chrysantas translated while

1   An ancient Persian unit of distance about four miles.

looking back at the man in the boat. He was wearing a cloak and it was hard to see his face, but the voice was familiar. Beggars were gathering ashore. "Marduk, bless you, grand masters—give to the poor," a beggar said.

Shoving his way clear, a procurer came forward and displayed a bronze emblem before their eyes to show he provided registered temple prostitutes. He knew the outsiders always had a few gold coins to spare for pleasure. "How about a wonderful night with girls from the temple before you start your trade, mister?" the man asked. Cyrus pushed him away, and told one of his companions to distribute some coins among the beggars. The procurer immediately identified Cyrus as the authority in the group. He stayed close to them, seeking an opportunity to sell his services.

The man in the cloak approached Chrysantas. Earlier he had offered to exchange their money on the canal. Chrysantas reached for his sword.

"There is no need for your blade, my friend," the man whispered, "have your eyes on the pimp—he is Nabonidus' watchdog."

"Behold, for I know you," Chrysantas shouted.

The man hushed him and gestured two of his companions to get rid of the pimp. They closed in on him and started a conversation. The pimp thought they were the newcomer's friends and started conversing with them. The man in the cloak pulled them away from the crowd, removed his head cover. Everyone was surprised to see Laban.

"I was hoping you would recognize me from my voice, commander," he said.

"Laban! What are you doing here?" Chrysantas said surprisingly.

Laban made a hush gesture. "It's dangerous to talk here," he said. "Follow me to an eatery—we can talk there."

The Ishtar gate was very crowded and the guards did not pay much attention to the newcomers. They followed Laban through the winding alleys of the Jewish quarter until they reached a tavern with an adjoining lodge. Laban paused for a few seconds and made sure nobody was following them. The custodian escorted them to a private room. Once inside, Laban breathed a sigh of relief and hugged everyone passionately. Then bowing before Cyrus, he said:

"What brings you here? You have taken a great risk coming into Babylon, my lord.

"Please address me like a regular citizen. We do not want to raise suspicion." Cyrus said. "Besides, we worried when we did not hear from you and Dara. And I also wanted to see the city before the operations."

"Well, your concerns are justified," Laban answered. Many things happened after I left your camp to come here; Artacamas tried to poison me on our way to Babylon when he found out about my mission."

Chrysantas' eyes widened. "He seemed to be a loyal soldier and I never suspected him," he said.

"He had hideous intentions though. Sent to your camp by Croesus before the Battle of Pteria, he was to assassinate Cyrus."

"How did you get all that information?" Chrysantas asked.

"Well, it's a long story. Artacamas told me all that after poisoning me in a lodge on our way," Laban answered. "He left me there, thinking I was about to die. Luckily, I had the right drug in my bag."

"And what cure saved you from a deadly poison?" Chrysantas

asked.

"Opium, my friend—is the antidote to most poisons. Mix a little with water and drink." He laughed loudly, "not more than the size of a black bean, though."

"What came of Dara?" Cyrus asked.

"Artacamas reported her on his arrival; she was arrested and sent to the dungeon in Nabonidus' palace."

"We have camped out of Babylon," Chrysantas said, "and it is crucial we take you and Dara back to our camp. Your information is essential for our plan of attack and operations inside Babylon."

"My sources say she has been taken to the Tower of Babel. She will be forced to spend the night with the high priest. Then she will be handed to the lower clerics to be prepared for sacrifice before the statue of Marduk[1] during the New Year's feast tomorrow."

"Where is the temple and is there any access other than the main gate?" Cyrus asked.

"It is near Ishtar gate," Laban answered. "a square building with a ziggurat[2] in the midst, measuring seven chebels[3] in breadth and length. It is also called the Gate of God with six towers and a large chamber on top. The tower bases become smaller as you move towards the summit. A flight of stairs running around the towers lead to the chamber."

"The outer access is well-guarded, but there is a secret stairway

---

1   Marduk: The ancient God of Babylon. Patron deity of Babylon.

2   An ancient Mesopotamian temple tower consisting of a lofty pyramidal structure built in successive stages with outside staircases and a shrine at the top (Merriam Webster).

3   Chebel: Ancient Persian unit equal to 100 feet.

within the tower walls. It is used only by the high priest to go back and forth to the chamber. Its entryway is inside the temple, someplace behind the altar. I have a friend, a freeman who works there. He will take us from waterways under the temple to the secret stairway. If everything goes well, we will be able to free Dara before dawn," Laban concluded.

*****

Dara had heard about the golden chamber and the story of the God of Babylon residing there. She knew that the priests of the temple prepared beautiful girls for the God who spent the night with them, and the poor girls were sacrificed the following day. She was reviewing her memories while they were dressing her up for the occasion. She had been planning to escape from the moment she was arrested. Having worked in the temple was an advantage. She was familiar with the chambers and labyrinths leading to underground canals and outlets. She had learned about the temple's secret doors and passageways when she was serving the queen. She always accompanied her to the temple, especially when she met the high priest confidentially.

The group dressing her for the occasion finished their work and were replaced with a make-up team. Then she was taken to the chamber on top of the seventh tower. The room was large. There was a couch in the center near a golden table. There were wide windows on either side, overlooking the whole city of Babylon.

"No slave girl has ever had the honor to serve the God in this chamber," the Chaldean[1] priest said. He fetched a goblet from a cupboard and handed it to Dara. "Drink this and you will spend the most wonderful night of your life here."

1 From Chaldea, which was a marshy land located in southeastern Mesopotamia.

Dara looked at him with suspicion and refused the goblet.

"Don't be afraid. I wouldn't dare harm you. The most precious wine for the most precious slave in Babylon," he said tasting the wine. Then, he left the goblet on the golden table and headed for the door.

Dara inspected the door as soon as he left the room. It was locked from behind. She went to the window. Far below her feet, the city was wide awake. They were preparing for the New Year's ceremony. She heard a noise from behind, turned, and there he was—the legendary God of Babylon. He was clad in a long purple broidered and decorated robe and wore a golden mask to match other objects in the chamber. She was surprised because the man seemed to have materialized from nowhere. *There must be a secret door*, she thought. Yet, she pretended to be fascinated by his sudden appearance. The man sat down on the couch and looked at her from behind the motionless mask. To her, he did not look like a God, nor did he act as one. He held on to the furniture as he moved. He sounded drunk when he told her to remain seated.

He approached and grabbed her hand. She tried to ward the man off, but his hands seemed to be made of steel. She decided to surrender to his wishes until she found a way out. As she lessened her resistance, he eased his grip but kept advancing. She fought back until she was exhausted and about to submit when she felt the overwhelming weight of the priest was removed from her body. She got up and to her surprise Laban was holding a sword at the neck of the high priest who was lying flat on the floor. His mask was off and Dara recognized his face. She had met him in the company of the queen many times.

Chrysantas, Laban, and their other companions talked in private for a few minutes. Then they had the priest sit on the couch while

Laban explained to him that soon Babylon was going to be captured by the Persian Army, and Nabonidus could not offer any serious resistance.

"You know that Cyrus is the most gracious of all conquerors. He is also respectful to all religions," Laban told the priest.

The priest nodded in confirmation. Astounded by the sudden appearance of the rescue party, Dara stared at the man with average height, soft black hair, penetrating eyes, and a hawk nose. Everyone kept silent when he talked. He returned her gaze with a pleasant, assuring smile. From his noble behavior and the descriptions in Hebrew society, she realized she was facing Cyrus, the legendary King of Persia.

"You are going to need his support when Babylon falls," continued Laban. "Besides, you do not want to be left at the mercy of the beggars and lepers at the Kebar Canal, do you?" He tapped the priest on the shoulder. "The filth in the canal and the disease of the plague-ridden slaves is going to kill you before the starving occupants tear you apart."

"The power of all deities is united in Bel-Marduk," said the priest. "King Cyrus can bring back the glories of the temple. I will prepare the priests and elders for his divine leadership."

*****

The avenues around the Esagila1 Temple were swarmed with the inhabitants of Babylon. It stood high in splendor with the gleaming tip above its rising tower. Everyone had come to join the New Year's Feast—even the slaves accompanied their masters. Royal guardsmen had been positioned along the avenues leading to the

---

1   A temple dedicated to Marduk, the patron god of Babylon.

temple. The crowd pushed against the backs of the guardsmen. The procession formed by the priests of Esagila Temple marched behind the statue of Bel-Marduk carried by the Hebrew slaves. A tablet from carnelian[1] stone carrying Nabonidus' prophecy, was being carried behind the statue. *At my feet, Cyrus will beg for mercy*, it said. It was going to serve him two purposes. If his son, Belshazzar, won the war against the Persians, the credit would go to him, for he had prophesied it. It would also raise the morale of his military against the Persians. Yet, the better-informed priests of Marduk noted otherwise. The words and rumors spreading among the slaves and the poor, who lived by the canal, were getting out of control. They no longer whispered the rumors about the coming of Mashiach, but openly talked of Cyrus' imminent arrival in Babylon.

Chrysantas and his companions pushed their way through the crowd and out of the city. Once on the other side of the canal, they uttered a sigh of relief and mounted their horses.

---

1   A brownish-red mineral which is commonly used as a semi-precious gemstone.

`

Chapter 17

The Messiah

Cyrus had already thought of an effective tactic to conquer Babylon without a bloody battle. Yet, he did not hesitate to seek the opinion of his allies. Led by his son, Cambyses, they had all joined forces with him from the remote corners of his empire. The Persian army bore colorful flags of different satrapies[1] and diverse uniforms

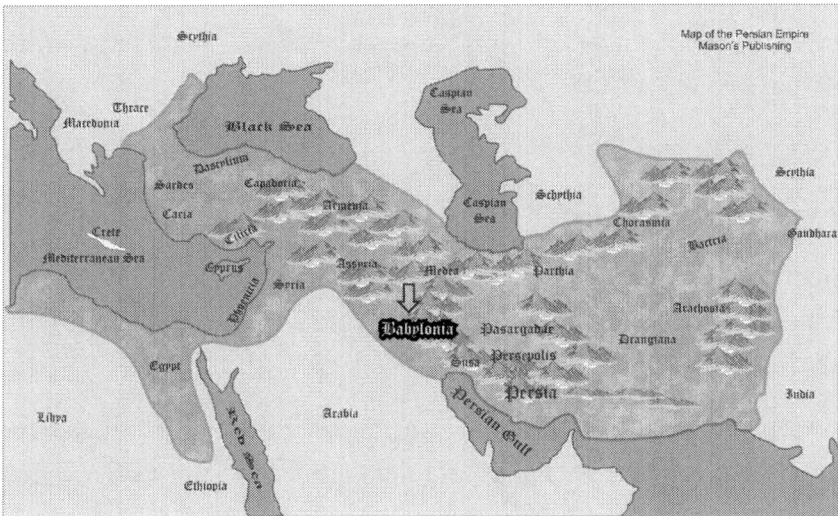

1   A province governed by a satrap.

in divisions made up of various nations. The Medes in leather skirts, loose tunics, and felt hats of various colors representing their ranks and classes. They carried javelins, bows and arrows, and short swords. The Persians in short tunics, fluted hats, loose-fitting robes with flowing sleeves, and baggy pants that allowed full movement of their arms and legs during the battle. They also carried javelins, long shield and long swords. Other nations included Armenians with shining helmets led by Tigranes, Parthians of the east, and Hyrcanians of the northeast. Elamites of Susiana, led by Gubaru, carried leather shields, kilts, and spears. Five thousand armored riders with lances and bows on armored chargers had joined the eternal guard.

Cyrus had ruled out taking the city through direct assault. He believed the fortification was too strong and would cost many lives to break through it. "Besides, a victorious, angry army would be blood thirsty," he said.

"That leaves us only one alternative," Gubaru said. "we set up a blockade and wait for Belshazzar to confront us in the open plains."

"A waste of precious time," Harpagus interrupted, "our men will grow impatient and lose their motivation. We do not know when Belshazzar will attack."

"Or if he will ever risk coming out of that fortress," Cyrus said. "now that our allies inside the city are preparing to help us, we have to come up with some wise idea of how to enter the city without force." He looked at the map on the table. The Euphrates River entering the city and its surrounding canals had been drawn with blue sand.

"The river divides the city into two parts—" Chrysantas said, "the palace is in the west part and the temple is in the east. We need not worry much about the temple side because our allies are there. Most of the slaves, however, are in the west section. They will join us as soon as we enter the city."

"How wide and deep is the river entrance?" Harpagus asked.

"It is about two men deep and four furlongs wide," Laban answered.

"While waiting for Belshazzar to attack, we will have our men dig a canal to divert Euphrates toward the low plains in the east," Cyrus said. "Then a group of our best men can enter the city through shallow waters and open the gate. We will occupy the city with no bloody conflict."

Outside the tent, the rising moon was spraying pale blue light on the plains of Babylon. Belshazzar was watching from the outskirts of the city. The Persian army campfires stretching to infinity made him fearful about the imminent confrontation. His father had been persuading him to march beyond the walls of the city and assault the enemy forces. "Teach Cyrus a lesson—humiliate him," he would say with passion. Cyrus, however, had already won the favor of the farmers and inhabitants of the towns and villages in the vicinity of Babylon. He paid for their crops with gold shekels brought from Sardis and kept the toll-takers away from the canals. Now the farmers could take as much water as they wished for their fields. "Hail, Cyrus!" They would shout at Belshazzar's men, "now our families can eat."

They called him the Law-Bearer. "The powerful shall not suppress the poor and powerless—this is our law," Cyrus had said to the town elders while his men were working along the river embankment and the maze of canals passing through farms ending at the marshlands further southeast. The peasants thought they were setting up traps to defend against surprise attacks by Belshazzar. Observing the sizeable army of the Persians, Belshazzar preferred to return into the city and defend from there.

After nightfall, the Persian army split up and approached two positions—the entrance and exit of the Euphrates River, led by Harpagus and Gubaru[1], respectively. Many soldiers were carrying short ladders, hidden by the cover of night from the eyes of Babylonian guards on top of the walls and watchtowers.

The wall ſtood high—a dark, menacing barricade towering toward the heavens. An outsider would have laughed at them carrying such small ladders compared to the high walls. The roaring torrents at the river entrance and exit posed a threatening barricade.

The guards at Ishtar gate watchtowers, near the river inlet, reported the enemy's activities close to the wall. At the river outlet, on the opposite side of the city, however, the movements of the Persian army went unnoticed because the guards did not watch those impassable marshy areas.

The wall commander looked through a crenel[2] trying to find out if there were any plot in progress that could threaten the city. Far below, the Persians were gathering at the wall. It was dark, and he could only see the silhouette of the men near the canal. Strong winds moved his cloak back and forth and obscured the vision of the guard beside him.

Far away from the city, men were at work by the river embankment. Cyrus was personally watching the operation. The thick embankment of the river wall, made of cement and bitumen, was hard to break. By midnight they had hardly made any significant progress. Every few minutes messengers arrived with news from the front. The army had taken up position.

"It is getting too late," Cyrus said. "if we don't make a sizable

1   Governor of Susiana.

2   An indentation in the battlements of a fort or caſtle, used for shooting or firing missiles through.

break in the embankment a few hours before sunrise, the whole plan will fail."

"It even endangers the army by the wall," Araspes said, "they won't have any protection once discovered in the morning."

"Catapult!" Cyrus shouted. "We can break the embankment by catapults."

The first few whistling stones passed above the barrage wall and dropped into the roaring river. The operators corrected the aiming device on their contraption and fired again. Huge projectiles started pounding the embankment repeatedly. After a number of direct hits, the strong structure gave in. A vast part of the wall came down, free-ing large bodies of water seeking escape. The river was returning to its original course as if it had never flowed toward the city of Babylon. The canals in the southeast of the city were overflowed. The dead lagoon quenched its thirst as the cold water flowed into it.

At the city wall, the fast moving river suddenly lost all its might and the level of water went down. The roaring of the river entering the city subsided. The commander on top of the wall took it for the autumn drought and the strong gust carrying the sound away. Yet, those black spots moving around hurriedly worried him.

"What could they possibly be up to?" he asked the guard beside him. His words were lost within the wailing of the wind lashing his cloak in the guard's face. The question remained unanswered.

"Whatever it is, we will know in the morning," he said, answer-ing his own question. *I have to report this to Belshazzar though,* he thought.

*****

The water was waist high now—perfect for their plan. The division commanders shouted orders and the soldiers jumped down into the river in great numbers. They entered the city through the river entrance in a matter of minutes. Small ladders were set up at the canal walls and the army stormed the areas in the vicinity of the river entrance. Soon, the Ishtar gate was opened to the Persian army. Other gates, including the ones at the river outlet, were also conquered and opened. By daybreak, the whole city was under control.

Belshazzar lifted his head from the soft pillow and looked at the crowd. Everything was hidden behind a membrane created by intoxication. His worries had gone away. Yet, the fearful face of the officer, who had brought the news from the wall, haunted his mind. *The Persians are at the wall.* Belshazzar laughed at him. *What possible threat could they pose,* he had thought. "Your concern is absurd," he had said to the officer, "watch them closely and wait until daybreak."

Dancers were twisting and turning with no apprehension of the imminent war. The slaves were moving confidently with their eyes glittering in joy—they all knew about the coming of the liberator. *The Persians called him Father and the Jews addressed him as the Anointed of the Lord.* Belshazzar recalled Isaiah 45:1-3. He had read it so many times that he could clearly review it in his mind with ease. *"Thus says the Lord to his anointed, to Cyrus, whom he has taken by his right hand to subdue nations before him and strip the loins of kings, to force gateways before him that their gates be closed no more: I will go before you levelling the heights. I will shatter the bronze gateways, smash the iron bars. I will give you the hidden treasures, the secret hoards, that you may know that I am the Lord.[1]"*

His thoughts were interrupted by vague figures entering the ceremony. They were clad in battle armor. The chaotic clamor of the

1   Isaiah 45:1-3.

feast suddenly stopped, and the crowd burst into a confused panic. Women screamed hysterically, and men were paralyzed in surprise. He did not believe his eyes. The newcomers wore crenelated hats. *The Persian soldiers,* he thought rubbing his eyes to make the nightmare vanish. Yet, the scene prevailed. A rush of adrenaline filled his body. He rose from his throne, hands shaking from fear and rage. He unsheathed his sword and charged with a circular motion to keep the enemy away. The Persians held a defensive stance and did not retaliate.

"We have our orders to treat you with respect," an officer said in Babylonian tongue. His voice carried no threat.

"Who are you people—where are my guards?" asked Belshazzar controlling his rage.

His guard commander, accompanied by two enemy soldiers, came forward. "The city has fallen to the Persian army," he said. "There is no point in resistance, my lord." His bloody arms showed he had been engaged in fighting.

Belshazzar lowered his sword and said, "I hope my family is safe."

"All Babylonian citizens, including the royal family, are under the protection of his Lordship, King Cyrus," the officer said. He disarmed Belshazzar and escorted him out along with four soldiers.

Chapter 18

Human Rights Declaration

Through the Ishtar Gate appeared Lord Cyrus on the twenty-ninth day of Tishrei[1] to bestow his blessings upon Babylon, scribed the chroniclers of Esagila Temple.

Cyrus liberates the Jewish slaves

1   Babylonian month coinciding with parts of September and October.

During the following days, the city was prepared for Cyrus"
public appearance. A day before the march, all nobles and high officials were given special robes and a rehearsal was conducted.
Pheraules, the imperial master of ceremonies, directed the practice
until he was satisfied. He had a good taste for beauty, and Cyrus
had personally ordered him to apply his special talent to make the
upcoming ceremony the most impressive of all. The ceremonial garments were mostly colored royal purple, blue, and luminous crim-
son blended with green.

The march began before sunrise. In the immediate precincts of
the royal palace, the Babylonian nobility were waiting to pay respect
to the new king. The sides of the road leading from the palace were
crowded with people waiting to see the legendary King Cyrus. The
immortals[1] cavalry directed the procession. They were followed by
the infantry of the Persians, the Medes, and other allies. The golden
rays of the freshly risen sun, reflecting from the shields and armors,
added a magical glory to the parade. They were followed by the
chariots riding on either side of the avenue. In the center, healthy
bulls and beautiful stallions, offerings to the Babylonian Gods, pre-
ceded strong men carrying a massive bronze container blazing with
eternal fire.

The palace gates opened and Cyrus joined the parade with
Gubaru riding at his side. He was wearing a light crown and garments of various shades of purple, scarlet, and royal blue. The crowd
bowed, watching in awe. Hundreds of lancers, archers, spearmen,
and mounted mace-bearers followed. They trailed Cyrus in divisions
comprised of the Medeans, Armenians, Hyrcanians, and other allies.
Upon arriving in the sacred precincts, Cyrus climbed the platform
set up on the first floor of the tower. Interpreters and narrators had
been positioned all over the vast square, and scribes wrote his decree

1   10,000 imperial guards existing in Persia under the Achaemenean dynasty.

in the Persian, Akkadian, and Elamite languages.

"People of Babylon," he began, "a few days ago, I walked in your streets, observed your ruler conduct, and talked to some of the citizens."

The crowd murmured in astonishment.

"In Persia, we are brought up to respect good thoughts, good speeches, and good deeds—the simple principles that every decent citizen respects."

"To us, a slave, an ox, and a cypress beam, as the temple managers have been administering, do not have the same value. As of now, all slaves are free citizens and like other people, they have the right to live anywhere they wish, and worship any god they prefer."

The crowd shouted in agreement.

"The temple holds the exclusive right to store, use, and rent the iron plows," he said, "we remove this right and from now on all farmers have the right to have iron plows—as many as they can use."

There was cheering in the crowd that would not subside, even if Cyrus raised his hand for silence. It took a while before he could talk again.

"To farmers, the flow of water is as necessary as the light from the sun. We remove the tax on water for irrigation. The water must flow free to fertilize the seeds that grow to nourish man and animal."

The cheering returned. People were excited and would not stop hailing when there were pauses.

"We have never practiced slavery. Selling men and women is prohibited in our kingdom, and we are going to exterminate such a tradition all over the world. I repeat, there is no justification for unpaid labor and hereafter all slaves are free."

He paused again, for this time slaves raised their voices, hailing and dancing happily everywhere among the crowd.

"They are free to return to their Holy Land," he continued, "and we shall help them repair their ruined cities and rebuild their temple. Slave dealers must now seek other productive trades. This is my command and this must be done."

Then he stretched out his hand toward the temple and said, "Marduk, the great lord, gave me his blessings and affected the heart of Babylonians in my favor to help me enter the city without a battle and catch the arrogant Nabonidus. From now on, all citizens are free to choose their faith and free to speak their minds, and those who deny them this right will be persecuted severely."

At this time, the procession of clerics, led by the high priest of Esagila Temple, started marching toward the imperial pavilion. They regarded Cyrus as if they were in the presence of a supreme being. The high priest of the Esagila Temple called him the embodiment of Bel-Marduk. They brought offerings, including slaves of different origin, whom Cyrus readily freed. He paid respect to Bel-Marduk in Akkadian language, surprising the clerics and officials who thought the language was confined to the celebrants of Marduk sanctuary. The high priest had arranged a ceremony to pronounce Cyrus as the patron saint of the temple. Cyrus refused the hand-kissing as part of the ceremony and announced that such practices destroyed human integrity and encouraged cowardice. He also condemned titles that connected him with prophets, gods, and other deities. He said it would induce the leaders to believe in having unlimited powers and turn them into tyrants.

After this ceremonial procession, Cyrus turned his attention back to the crowd that was eager to hear more from him.

"No religion has superiority over others," he said. "They all mean to spread good values, yet greedy clergymen tend to turn them into profitable business. The great Zoroaster says, 'One good deed is worth a thousand prayers.'"

He paused. There was chatter among the priests.

"Beware of false prophets. Stop being naive devotees. I respect your right to follow the faith of your choice, yet believe that no religion is perfect without encouraging good thought, good speech, and good deed—the three simple messages that promote happiness, freedom, and prosperity for all. Defend your freedom by preserving your right to think and question the priests and rulers. They tend to unite in order to deny your liberty."

The crowd burst into spontaneous cheers as soon as he paused for breath.

"Beware of religious groups representing a vengeful God. They have strong ties with Ahriman[1], feed on ignorance and spread lies. They kill non-believers and rape women in their captivity. Ask them if they honor *Love* and *Chivalry*. They do not—for Ahriman is devoid of such values. They hate the truth and long for hypocrisy and flattery. Insincere compliments fill them with joy and give them the feeling of false importance. They are cowards and hide among women and children, fearing to face real warriors. They are wolves in sheep's clothing. But remember, my children, only your fear makes them look bigger. Fear not these tyrants, and you will bring them down with a strong will."

The crowd cheered while he came down from the tower and headed for the palace. His decree was written in three languages. It

1   A Persian word for Lucifer.

was then transferred to a clay cylinder, backed and placed above the temple gate.

During the following days, he humbly appeared in public, stopped at different places, and told entertaining stories. The farmers, scholars, artisans, and other classes of people put forth arguments in which he participated. He even took part in dialogue among the beggars of the canal. His army commanders were ordered to employ Babylonian warriors of all ranks and specialties. They were given the choice of remaining in their regiments or delivering their weapons to start other professions. Many of them chose to remain and serve in the Persian army.

Cyrus had made a pledge to liberate the Jews. The task was not so easy to fulfill. They had been away from their land for generations. Setting them free was not enough. It would take incredible effort and resources to accomplish the undertaking. He assembled a large group, including experts from all walks of life, to help organize the exodus of the slaves back to their land. Laban and Dara helped him find the appropriate people who could lead. He also appointed many of his army officers and warriors to protect the migrating Jews back to Jerusalem. They guarded multiple wagons, loaded with gold and silver to help the liberated slaves build their temples and towns. Many Jewish people chose to migrate to live in Persia or serve in the Persian army.

*****

The conquest of Babylon was a major achievement for Cyrus. He had great ambitions for improving the lifestyle throughout his empire. The following spring, he appointed Gubaru as the governor of Babylon and returned to Pasargadae to oversee his kingdom. For a few years, he exerted himself in the service of the citizens. He had to serve them as their *father,* making certain that his subordinates gave to the people rather than taking away from them.

Chapter 19

The Massagetai

News from the north was disappointing. The Hyrcanian satrap reported the onset of attacks on the northern towns and villages by Massageteans[1]. Cyrus recalled venturing in those areas along with Abradates a long time ago. They were hunting hogs in that region

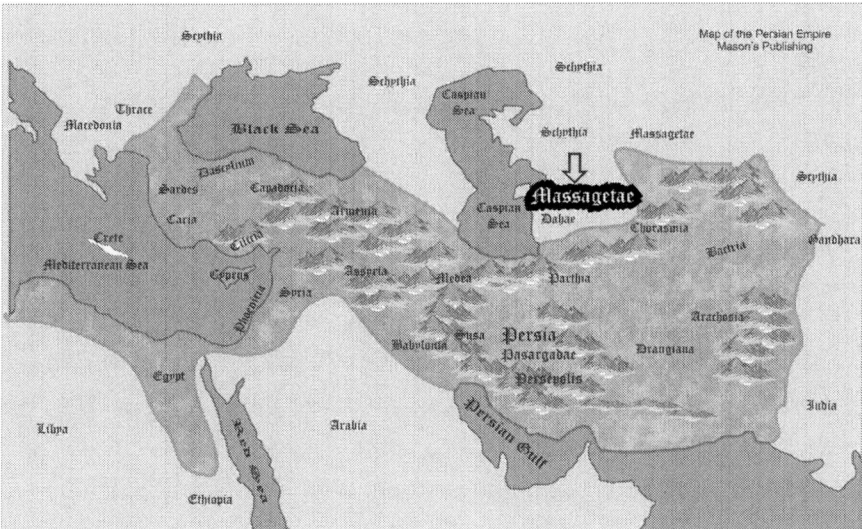

1   Huns.

when attacked by two Massagetai wolves—a name given to them by locals to mean mythical creatures that were swift and savage like wolves. Cyrus held a meeting with his generals to discuss options against the Massagetai. All his men including Tigranes, the Armenian, and Diodotus, the representative of Hyrcanian Satrap, were present.

"Long time since our last campaign in Babylonia," Cyrus began. "Apart from small revolts and riots, we have not had any major challenging forces threatening our satrapies since then."

He paused and picked up a small object before him on the table. The audience became curious. It looked like an arrowhead made of brass.

"Diodotus removed this arrowhead from his herder's back—only Massagetai make their arrowheads from brass. They stole 200 lambs from the herdsman killed by this arrow."

Everyone reacted in defiance.

"No wonder they call that region the wolf land," Harpagus said.

"You said it, General Harpagus—the Massageteans are truly wolf-like when it comes to lifestyle," Diodotus said, "and the real wolves also come from their land into our territories."

Cyrus then invited the audience to listen to Diodotus' account of the Massageteans.

"The Massageteans are a tribe of Scythians who live beyond the Araxes River," Diodotus said, "they also live in the western borders of the Sea of Caspian. They worship the sun, share their wives, and have sex in the open. To them, dying in bed is a dishonor. They prefer to die in battle or offer themselves for sacrifice in old age. Their bodies are then eaten by their heirs who believe they would take after their ancestors by doing so. Farming is not popular among them, so they live on their herds and the fish of the Caspian Sea and Araxes River, over which we have dispute with them. They are brave warriors who know the art of fighting, both on horse and on foot. They are skilled in using lances and bows, yet their favorite weapon is the battle-axe. Their sword and other weapons, including their breastplate, is made of brass and less likely to be broken. They shape their arrowheads from gold or brass, for they do not have iron mines in their land or aware of the art of trade with other nations. They are all loyal to Queen Tomyris, ruling their land at present. Recently, they have increased their attacks on our villages and taken to plunder and theft. All our attempts to bring them to their senses through negotiations have failed, and we think there is no alternative other than going to war against them."

"They have started the offensive attacks in our territories; we have enough reason to march against them," Cyrus interrupted. "Of course, we are not going to prepare a big army, because they are just groups of savages and the art of tactical war is unknown to them."

He then adjourned the meeting until General Harpagus prepared an army for the task with the help of Cambyses who was learning the techniques of war under his supervision.

Chapter 20

The march against Massagetai

The royal pavilion had been pitched on top of a hill, overlooking the Araxes River. From there, Cyrus observed the undergoing bridge operation on the river. The spirit of craftsmanship and production had returned to the warriors. On both sides, they were building boat-like structures, which formed the cross-beams of a huge bridge. The smooth ripples of water were spreading across the river. The reflection of the rainforest was dancing on the ridges of those tiny waves. *Once I am done with this task, I must stay in Pasargadae and concentrate more on internal affairs—more facilities for farmers, herders, and educators.* At the threshold of the royal stable, down the hill, a man currycombing horses was also looking at the river with a wide grin across his face. If Laban or Croesus had been there, they would have recognized Artacamas immediately.

Tigranes was approaching the royal pavilion. He was the commander of the Armenian legion. When he was young, he had taken a trip to Massagetae and lived there for a while. His father had established a good relationship with them and wanted Tigranes to socialize and learn their culture. Now that they were about to confront them in war, Cyrus was seeking his advice about the traditions, ethics, and cultural behavior of his enemy.

The guards let Tigranes through. He entered the tent, saluted Cyrus, and waited to be spoken to.

"I hope your legion is in high spirits, Tigranes—is there anything you need?" asked Cyrus.

"Everything is fine, my lord," said Tigranes. "Our warriors are ready for the battle."

"I was told you experienced living among the Massagetai a long time ago," Cyrus said.

Tigranes' eyes lost focus, as if he were visualizing some event on an unknown horizon.

"Now that we are planning to attack them, your experience might be of utmost help," Cyrus added inviting him to sit down at the table in one corner.

"Yes, my lord," Tigranes answered, recalling his observations.

"I had just turned 22," he began, "when my father sent me to the Massagetai Court for a visit. We sailed across the Caspian Sea to reach their land. I had been told to watch intently and learn about the culture and tradition of the people. Prince Spargapises was a young teenager then. He was my guide as we traveled in the countryside through their land. While hunting in the outskirts of the town, we stopped in a village. We took our kill to a family who was friends with Verixom, the son of one of the generals. Our hosts prepared the kill for dinner while we were drinking. Right before sunset, everyone gathered in front of the house. The meat was set up to roast, and we kept drinking and socializing with our hosts around the fire. Everyone was carrying some kind of a green fruit the size of pears in their hands. They kept throwing the fruit in the fire. It cracked and produced a smoke with a good smell and an intoxicating effect. There were many beautiful women in their family. One of them paid special attention to me. I found out that she was the bride of the youngest son in the family."

"Do you want to have sex with her?" Verixom murmured behind my ear.

"Well, she is married to the youngest son of this family, isn't she?" I answered.

"Yes," Verixom said, "but still, it would be all right if you like her—I see she pays special attention to you."

"How could you say that?" I asked him. "They are your friends, after all."

"Well," Verixom laughed, "you do not know of our tradition. We only marry one woman, yet we hold all our wives in common. Once you like a woman, you can hang your sword at their door and enter her bedroom with permission. They would be honored. The woman must also agree with your courtship though. That is all there is to it."

"I thought it was a strange tradition, because in our country the act would have been considered a sinful behavior."

Tigranes paused for a few moments, sipping on the drink Cyrus had offered him. Then he continued his story.

"I have another memory from my trip that brings shivers to my spine," he continued. "Once, we were staying in a village near the shores of the Caspian Sea. Caviar fish was abundant and an easy catch. One morning, my companions said we were invited for a sacrifice ritual. Around mid-day the crowd gathered in the village square. Everyone was happy, drinking and dancing. Early evening,

a group of people approached the square with colorful flags and to-
tems carried by their youngsters. They came to a halt in the middle
of the square and led an old man to a prepared platform. At first, I
thought they were going to offer the sacrifice to the old man. Later
on, however, I was horrified to find out that the old man himself was
the target of the sacrifice. He was given some drink that apparently
made him ecstatic. He was in a state of trance when a young man
went to his side, kissed him, and placed a short sword in his hand.
He stood up and gave a cry of ecstasy raising his sword. Then the
young men of the family approached and slaughtered him with their
weapons. The man did not suffer much because they all targeted his
heart. Moments later, he lay there dead on the platform.

I was shocked and asked my companion why they did that. He
said the old man had an honorable death while holding a sword and
symbolically died in a fight and the fact that not all old men in the
tribe would have a chance to die in such a fashion. He explained
to me that when the elders of a family reach old age, they offer
themselves for sacrifice before they become disabled and turn into
a hangdog. The members of the family, then gather together in a
ceremony and sacrifice him. Afterwards, they cook his flesh and everybody eats it, for they believe that the spirit, bravery, and experience of the sacrificed man would thus reincarnate in his children and
grandchildren and whoever else consumes that flesh. Those who die
in sickness lose the opportunity to continue living in the bodies of
their children. They will be cast to purgatory and will have to spend
a boring afterlife for eternity.

The family of the dead man were busy cutting and cleaning his
flesh. They put the pieces in a big pot containing boiling water. They
added different herbs and seasoning and continued drinking and
dancing until late evening. Then everyone was given a share of the
flesh. I was honored to be given a piece for which I had to express

my gratitude. I pretended to eat, but buried it in the ground as I wandered away from the crowd."

"Strange tradition," Cyrus said, "—they have some rationality in their practice though, through this practice, they avoid the costly expenses of caring for their elders when they get sick."

"Yes, my lord, and they even follow a surprisingly aggressive tradition when war breaks out," Tigranes answered.

Cyrus smiled as he watched the work in progress across the river. He seemed to have guessed what Tigranes was about to say.

"At wartime," he continued, "these old people, including the ones who are still strong, volunteer to march before the younger and stronger warriors."

"Think of so many fighters who have nothing to lose," Cyrus interrupted, "with one intention—killing the enemy at all cost. That would be an army of fierce warriors who fight like mad dogs. This would easily demoralize orderly warriors who are trained to fight tactical wars."

"Yes, my lord. That is what I have been thinking about for the last few days."

"Well," Cyrus said, "we have to come up with our own tactics to neutralize this threat. Avoid man-to-man confrontation and use an element of surprise."

Cyrus paused for a few moments as if unaware of his surroundings.

"What kind of weaponry do they use most, and do they have a sizeable cavalry?" he asked.

"No, my lord, they don't have a sizeable trained cavalry, but fighting on horseback is not strange to them. They fight in an erratic and disorderly fashion though. As for weapons, they favor the battle-axe, yet they use lances and bows when it comes to exchanging deadly arrows from a distance. They make their arrowheads of brass and gold."

"Golden arrowheads," said Cyrus, with a look of dramatic irony on his face.

"Spear points, as well. They have gold in abundance, and this metal is not so dear to them as it is to us," Tigranes answered.

As he was riding back to his legion, Tigranes noticed a delegation of Massagetai approaching the camp. *They must have an important message for Cyrus,* he thought.

*****

The royal pavilion was heavily guarded. Only generals were present. Croesus was also participating per Cyrus' order. Everyone rose from their seats as Cyrus entered the tent. He went straight to the head of the table and without any introduction, said:

"Tomyris has sent a delegation with offers. She says that we need to return to our country and live in peace."

"Apparently, she has forgotten about their permanent assaults at our borders, murdering our innocent farmers, and stealing herds from our territories," Diodotus said, "our villages are still burning and the survivors mourning the massacre of their loved ones."

"We will never have peace at our borders, unless she is subdued," Tigranes added.

There was a murmur of acknowledgment. Cyrus invited them to silence. "She has two more proposals—either we retreat three days from the border, and they will march to battle in our land or they retreat three days from the border, and we attack them there to settle our disputes."

"Either proposal is going to buy them three days to prepare for confrontation," Chrysantas said, "I suggest we pass the river and attack them right away—that would keep them from preparing for defense."

"Well," the Hyrcanian general said, "considering the front line of their army, the suicidal old, three days march into our mountainous territory is going to exhaust them of their energy and ready them for our blades."

"True," Harpagus said, "they are used to living in a flatland and marching in a mountainous terrain would be new to them. They do not know what lies in every corner of the gorges. We can, very well, unleash hell on them at every mountain path along the way. By the third day, when they arrive at our rendezvous, they will have already shrunken to a defeated army ready to negotiate a surrender."

"Besides, we have the advantage of knowing our territory very well and our warriors would be in high spirit because they will be fighting in their own country," the Hyrcanian general said.

"Well, we heard all about the advantages of retreating into our land." Everyone turned toward the speaker who had been silent all along. It was Croesus. "I believe the opposite, and I would present my reasons if my lord grants permission."

"We would be delighted to hear your opinion," Cyrus said. "You have the experience of leading a great country and an aggressive army."

"Retreating into our land would have many disadvantages," Croesus said. "First of all, it would psychologically dishearten our warriors, because not knowing about our tactics, they would think of it as a sign of weakness. Second, it would be a waste of time and provisions, as much as twelve days, if everything goes according to the plan. Three days to arrive here, three days to build the bridge, three days retreat, and three days waiting for the enemy to attack."

Looking at the generals Croesus was silent for a few seconds to weigh the effect of his logic on their faces. "Besides," he continued, "who can guarantee the Massagetai would ever attack as promised. Most important of all, if they attack and by some luck win the fight, they would be three days already into our territories and will be encouraged to ride along and conquer our cities, one after another, before an organized defense can be assembled. Probably, the whole empire would face the danger of collapse."

No one dared to challenge his argument. After a few moments, Cyrus broke the silence. "I have made arrangements for the major part of our army to be battle ready just in case we face any difficulties in this war. My son, Cambyses, will be in command and ready to join us if required." He looked at his generals to give them encouragement and confidence about the backup army.

"Considering all the arguments about the first choice, I agree with Croesus and Chrysantas, and would like all of you to prepare for an attack. General Harpagus and Chrysantas will be conveying my further instructions." Then he waved for Harpagus and Chrysantas to remain in the tent. The rest of the generals, including Croesus, left. Until very late, the three of them were discussing tactics of the upcoming battle. It was near the break of dawn when the generals left.

Chapter 21

An Abandoned Camp

Spargapises was puzzled. There was no activity in the camp. During the day, all his intelligences had reported the arrival of the Persian army and their encampment. Now, there were no souls to be seen in the camp. He sent a few men to investigate the possibility of a plot. They all returned with one answer. The Persians had evacuated in a hurry, leaving behind all that could slow them down. Most likely they had learned of his approaching army and retreated in a hurry because they were outnumbered or they could have agreed with his mother's suggestion and were retreating three days away from the borders. He sent his intelligences to follow their track. They were already far away. Their camp lights showed they were one day march away from the place. Such a delightful, early victory for Spargapises. Proudly, he moved through the camp and ordered his warriors to settle and stay for the night. The food, fruit, and wine left behind were so abundant that he could feed his warriors for a few days.

As he rode through the camp, he could see the signs of admiration in the eyes of his men. He had ordered that a generous portion of the food and wine be distributed among the tired warriors who were just settling around the campfires and already eating and drinking. There were cries of joy and satisfaction. This event would be a big credit for him among the army generals. Massagetai had heard that the Persians drank wine, yet they were not much aware of the properties of the drink. They did not know that wine was a slow acting drink, so they drank more and more to see how effective it was. Hours after midnight, they were deeply intoxicated. Spargapises was staggering and swaying as he walked through the camp. Looking at his men—drunk and helpless—he realized he had made a big mistake. *What if the enemy raids at this time,* he thought. *It would be a total failure. I won't live to regret it.*

A few hours past midnight the whole Massagetai warriors were asleep like gentle babies when the Persians came fast upon them. There was no serious defense and they fell prey to Cyrus. Spargapises was seized while trying to put the sword to himself. He was too drunk to even stab himself, let alone engaging in combat. Soon, he was at Cyrus' presence.

"You are going to be a disappointment to your mother, Spargapises," Cyrus said. "I hope she comes to her senses and seeks other remedies to this dispute, rather than battle."

"That was a dirty trick," Spargapises said somberly, "not expected from a man like you."

"I blame your behavior on the good wine you have drunk. Let's wait until you are sober tomorrow. Then we are going to decide what to do with you," Cyrus concluded. "keep him in confinement until he comes to his senses."

The following day, Tomyris sent herald saying that Cyrus could not take pride in the victory over a third of her army because the victory was not achieved through a battle but rather through a trick.

She then demanded that her son be freed, or she would have her revenge. Cyrus returned the herald ignoring her demand. Spargapises became sober when the wine left his system. He asked Cyrus to let him out of his chains and promised to behave. Cyrus ordered that he be released of his confinement. Once freed, he found a dagger and ended his own life. Cyrus sent a messenger to Tomyris with the account of the incident and his readiness to deliver the body to her, so that she could give him a proper burial. Tomyris sent an envoy under Verixom to escort the body of Spargapises back to their camp. Cyrus treated them very respectfully and appointed Tigranes to receive them. Tigranes welcomed Verixom warmly and helped him in the best possible way to accomplish his mission.

*****

The wagon was riding along a narrow forest road toward Tomyris' camp. The men escorting the wagon noticed a rider approaching from among the trees. Verixom shouted halt and prepared for confrontation in case of a trick. The approaching rider was Artacamas who demanded to talk with the commander alone.

"The reason I am here to talk with you is because I noticed you could speak our language when you talked to Tigranes," said Artacamas. "I do not want to disclose my name, for I will be executed if my identity is revealed," he added.

"Well, what is your business with us, though?" Verixom asked.

"I am the nephew of Astiages, the late Medean emperor and the brother-in-law of Croesus, the former emperor of Lydia. I sympathize with you, as your prince was killed through a plot by Cyrus. I am going to help your queen defeat him. If you follow my instructions, you will be able to identify and kill him during the upcoming battle."

There was a look of shock on Verixom's face. Deep inside he was disgusted by the man who was a traitor to his king. He had heard about Cyrus' good reputation and his chivalrous manners. Cyrus was his enemy, but he did not want him dead. Still, he had to report the incident to his higher officer. It could change the fate of the upcoming battle.

"What do you want me to do now?" Verixom asked.

"Well, tell your queen about my cause, and I will meet you in this spot the night before the battle," said Artacamas. "I will give you instructions on how to identify Cyrus among the warriors and arrange that his horse be crippled in the battleground. He is invincible while on his charger. You will know the details the night before the battle."

Verixom watched him ride away doubting if the man could be trusted. Cyrus had honored him as a respectable enemy warrior. He truly deserved his legendary reputation, and this inferior man was betraying him. Many noble heroes had been murdered because of treason, and he wondered if Cyrus was going to be another unlucky one. When all was said and done, he decided that he would not let Artacamas live.

Chapter 22

A Conspiracy

Before the break of dawn, Croesus woke up. He had a nightmare. He had seen Cyrus soaked in his blood. Even though he had been defeated by Cyrus and lived in captivity, every day he came to like him more and more. Long after he was defeated in Sardis, Cyrus had considered him as a family member and respected him very much and sought his advice when it came to making crucial decisions. And in this battle, he had given priority to his views over the other generals.

He was concerned because he had seen Artacamas around the stable a few times. At first, he thought it was just an illusion, but he saw him talking to one of the Massagetai when the body of their prince was being loaded onto a wagon. As he approached the wagon, Artacamas went away, trying to avoid confronting him. *He is up to something,* Croesus thought. And now this nightmare—he had to find out what Artacamas was plotting. He got up, dressed, and stepped out of his tent. He looked across the plain far below the hill. There was silence across the army tents. The campfires were still alive and twinkling in the avenues between the tents. His gaze absently stopped at the royal stable—he had seen Artacamas there most of the times. It was lit inside, more lit than just the night light. He knew there was some activity in progress inside.

First, he thought he would send for Chrysantas and tell him about his concern, but he thought it might just be some paranoid reaction and he'd better check first, before he panicked. He decided to go to the stable and inspect the activity there. As he sneaked into the stable, the horses became aware of some strange presence and stirred uneasily in their stalls. He hid behind haystacks and worked his way toward the shop and saddle hangers. With his back toward the entrance, Artacamas was busy with a saddle on an anvil. Croesus readily recognized Cyrus' saddle from its ornaments. Yet, he did not move and continued observation. Using a dagger, the man was carving small spots in the leather, pointing the sharp end of the scraped leather outward where it would touch the animal's back. Croesus noticed a small pouch by his side, which he recognized as the pouch of poison he had given to Artacamas, long before engaging in war against Cyrus.

After he was done, Artacamas opened the pouch, mixed the powder with a liquid, and smeared the whole back surface of the saddle with the liquid. Then he turned the saddle and, using a scraper, he started making tiny abrasions on top where it came in contact with the rider's thigh. Croesus was shocked at the idea. *He is going to cause gradual poisoning of the rider and the horse.* He felt an urge to rush out of the stable and inform Cyrus of the conspiracy. He knew he was not a match for Artacamas in case of a confrontation. He slowly moved out of his hiding to sneak back out of the tent. As he backed away, watching Artacamas, he came into contact with a horse. The animal reacted and uttered a neigh while standing on its hind legs. It struck Croesus' forehead instinctively, as it would strike an enemy on a battlefield. Croesus gave a loud cry and dropped unconscious before the horse. Frightened of discovery, Artacamas stopped working on the saddle and moved cautiously toward the stalls. Soon, he discovered the insensible body. He knew Croesus no longer approved of continuing grudge against Cyrus. During an accidental confrontation in Babylon, Croesus had told him to abandon the idea of harming Cyrus and serve him with honesty. At that time he had to hide his grudge, but now he wished to tell him that he took orders from his new master, Queen Tomyris. The daybreak was approaching and soon the stable master would come yelling at him to prepare for the battle. He tied up Croesus, covered his mouth, and tucked him away behind the haystacks at the far end of the stable. Soon, he would be gone and when his uncle was discovered, it would be too late. He had already informed Tomyris of his plot. He was ready to flee to the Massagetai camp as soon as Cyrus mounted his horse before the battle.

Chapter 23

The Final Confrontation

The Massagetai warriors had been pouring down from the surrounding hills since dawn. They pushed forward with an uncontrollable rage. In the heart of their army was Tomyris' legion, which looked more organized than the others. They encircled her division, as if her protection were their only concern. They moved in a disorderly fashion and most of them carried battle-axes. The organized part of the army wore light clothing with brass or gold breast-plates, reflecting blinding rays from the sun shining in the south. The front rows carried big, rectangular shields to protect themselves against the Persian arrowheads.

There was a chill in the air. Cyrus' horse moved uneasily as he approached the station at the foothill where he was going to address his army.

"Warriors of the Persian Empire," he began, "since our victory in the plain of Pasargadae, we have battled against many forces and brought down empires and tyrants all for one cause—liberty! The most important right worth dying for!" He paused, as the warriors army cheered with excitement. The officers and interpreters were translating his message far across the encampment.

"You are well aware that we are not here to invade another country. Our cause is ending an invasion. We came here to defend our countrymen who live at our borders and deserve to live in peace."

The warriors shouted in anger.

"Peace for farmers and herders who have repeatedly been oppressed by Massagetai. We are here to tell them we will no longer tolerate any plunder and robbery at our borders."

Shouts of acknowledgement rose across the army as he paused for his message to be carried to the remote parts of the army. He knew that his agents would spread the highlights of his message among the enemy warriors as well. He also knew that Tomyris had told her people that Spargapises had been murdered in captivity in order to awaken the spirit of revenge in them. That would give them more incentive to fight rather fiercely. Cyrus had to kill that spirit in them.

"You know that we are not killers of war prisoners—nor do we appreciate slavery in our land. Yet, we are disappointed in the Massagetai prince for committing suicide when he was set free in our camp as a gesture of our good intention—what a shame that a prince cannot tolerate defeat. To us, suicide is not an answer. We die turning our swords to our enemies—and that is what we are going to do today."

The whole army cheered with excitement, and he paused for the cheering and shouting to subside.

"We have defeated this enemy before, and, today, we are going to defeat them again."

The cheering took up again. His horse stirred in its place uneasily. He then faced the Massagetai lines, drew his two short swords and pointed them toward the enemy. The Persian warriors began clanging their swords on their shields. The overwhelming sound had a demoralizing effect on the enemy. The Massagetai returned the threat with cheering and jumping up and down in their places. Cyrus motioned by crossing his swords. The sky of the battlefield turned black with the archers' arrows. The enemy warriors raised their shields. Cries of agony and pain filled the enemy lines.

They returned the attack with their own arrows. The front rows of the Persian army were well-protected with long shields, and the Massagetai arrows hardly reached deeper into the Persian lines. There were occasional cries of pain. The archers from both sides continued firing arrows. The flow of arrows from the Persian side reduced as Cyrus brought the two points of his swords together. The enemy, however, kept shooting at full-force until exhausted.

For a few minutes, everything was quiet. Only the whistling of the cold wind mixed with the wailing of the wounded broke the silence. There were no more exchanges of arrows. On the Massagetai side, the warriors could not help raising their war cries. A command from Tomyris released them and they started charging toward the Persians. Cyrus remained on the hilltop and kept issuing commands with sign language.

All his divisions waited for the enemy to charge. As the Massagetai forces drew closer, the Persian archers broke into fierce activity again. The front suicidal rows of the enemy, charging blindly with no shield protection, were caught in surprise as deadly arrows brought them to their knees. Horses neighed and stumbled as arrows hit their bodies. The rows behind them stumbled upon them and more arrows from the Persian side brought the charging Massagetai rows to chaos. Then, upon Cyrus' command, the Persian army was mobilized and marched toward the disorderly enemy warriors. The Massagetai reorganized in the back rows and charged again. The battle continued for an hour and the Massagetai warriors who had initially advanced, gradually began to retreat. Throughout the fierce battle, however, a watchful observer would have noticed that occasionally some strong Massagetai warriors would drop dead, even without an injury or serious conflict.

Chapter 24

The Death of the Father

The Massagetai withdrawal continued, and Cyrus moved further toward the battlefield in order to keep communication with the commanders. As his charger galloped deeper into the battlefield, it started faltering while dragging its feet over the bodies. Cyrus ran his hand through its mane. Its body was cold and wet with sweat. He could feel its muscles quivering. He called out to one of the guards.

"Go to the stable and get me another charger. My horse is ill."

The guard left. He dismounted the horse. Things looked hazy. The horse's eyes were dull and blank. Cyrus felt dizzy and confused as well. He hung onto the horse's neck as the guards approached to help him. His feverish, glassy eyes swept the battleground around him.

The stable was deserted. Near the stalls, the guard discovered the body of the stable master—stabbed from behind. The stalls were all empty—no chargers left. Then he heard a noise and discovered Croesus tied up behind the haystacks. He told the guard that Cyrus' life was in danger and they had to warn him about the poison applied to the saddle by Artacamas.

Far away on the battleground, Cyrus knew some sinister act had crippled him and his horse. The horse had lost balance and was laying on the ground now. The enemy corpses were gradually res-urrecting from the dead in great numbers. A select vicious group of the strongest Massagetai warriors. In a matter of seconds they surrounded the guards who were quite outnumbered. Cyrus' guards fought with glory and passion to defend *the Father* and brought down many of the enemy warriors, before falling down themselves.

Cyrus was leaning against the horse with blank eyes. He was ob-serving the battle unfolding before his eyes. A few giant Massagetai warriors approached him. He concentrated all his strength, rose to his feet, and rotated on one foot to let the charging enemy pass him while thrusting an effective blow in his side. The man was thrown face-down in the mud and did not rise. Cyrus fought with both hands, defending with one hand and charging with the other. His opponents looked hazy, yet he accurately predicted their maneuvers and landed his blows in harmony with their moves. His enemies were strong but slow-moving, and Cyrus was fast and good in strike-and-dodge technique.

The increasing number of his foes, the effect of the poison, and the loss of blood from a number of wounds, finally brought him down to his knees. Fatigue and partial paralysis overcame. Far away, he could see a group of his warriors approaching, but he did not have the energy to hold on any longer. He still fought while on his knees. He felt the stabbings from enemy warriors on his side that was not protected by his breast-plate. Blood was running down his body. He turned and slashed at the man behind him with his last

strength. His sword slit the Massagetai's throat who lost balance
and fell upon Cyrus. He pushed the dead man away with a kick and
turned his sword to defend against another charging figure while
holding a third one by the neck with his other hand. A deadly blow
on his head turned everything black. He let go of the Massagetai's
neck, but kept his grip on the single sword upon which he was leaning. The freed man brought up his sword and thrust it in the side of
his neck. Cyrus took a last glimpse of his dying charger and fell on
the ground. *Poison is indeed the women's weapon*, he thought. The
Massagetai were already running away at the site of the approaching Persians. Croesus and the guard arrived first. Croesus got hold
of a spear and thrust it through the Massagetai's throat who was just
turning away from Cyrus' body. Chrysantas arrived with a group of
warriors behind him. Croesus was holding Cyrus' head on his lap.
Cyrus opened his eyes, took one last breath and died.

The account of the incident was soon circulated among the warriors. The battle, however, continued into the evening, until they
gradually retreated back to their own camps. Cambyses had arrived, and the Persians were now mourning the death of *the Father*.
Tomyris sent a herald, suggesting a cease-fire and her readiness for
a peace treaty. Verixom brought the head of Artacamas as a token of
their commander, for it was his betrayal that caused Cyrus' death.
Cambyses returned the head, stating that the traitor did not deserve
to be buried in Persia. He said he would discuss the cease-fire proposal and reach a decision the following day.

In the royal tent, the body of Cyrus rested on a bench while
Cambyses and the generals discussed their next move. Everyone believed they should agree to a treaty with the Massagetai and return
to their own land. The warriors were in low spirits and in no condi-
tion to carry out the battle in an effective manner. General Harpagus

also agreed on accepting the cease fire. Cambyses approved of the tactic and the following day there was a treaty signed by both sides. The Massagetai made a pact not to invade the Persian border towns again. The Persian army returned to Pasargadae and buried Cyrus in a tomb near his palace.

Epilogue

The golden rays of the scattering dawn penetrate through the surrounding thicket, seeking the disc on top of the monument. Evaporating dews reduce the rays to their underlying tints. A rainbow of heavenly colors surround the tomb. The simple inscription on the disc comes to life.

"O, Man, I am Cyrus who founded the Empire of the Persians and King of Persia. Grudge me not therefore this monument."[1]

Tomb of Cyrus The Great in Pasargadae

1   Reported by Strabo, the Greek Philosopher.

Within the top cavity of the megalith, rests the body of *the Fa-ther,* facing the heavens. The guardian angels[1] on its seven steps, as the ancient Persians would say, protect it from elemental and man-ual forces. Historical eras have passed and many warriors of noble origin visited his tomb. The Persians regarded him as the '*Father,*' the Babylonians as the '*Liberator,*' the Greeks as the '*Law-Giver,*' and the Jews as the '*Anointed of the Lord.*' Plato praised him as *the model of enlightened monarch.* The Shah of Iran regarded him as a *historical paradigm of the Persian dominion.* And Thomas Jeffer-son, the president of the United States, read his story in *Cyropedia*[2] and recommended his grandson to read it in his Greek studies.

Following the death of Cyrus the Great, the Iranians lived in glory and prosperity for 1200 years until the invasion of Arab Mus-lims in 642 AD[3] infected the Persians with a dark ideology that last-ed for more than 1400 years. During the secular Pahlavi Dynasty (1925-1979 AD), the country was advancing toward democracy and modernity when another deceptive incident stopped this promising progression. In 1979, a fanatic mullah named Khomeini convinced some of his followers to revolt and replace the Iranian secular gov-ernment with his falsely utopian regime that later proved to be a burning hell called The Islamic Republic, which threw Iran on a path to regression again.

Renaissance movements are now uniting the Iranians in-side and outside the country to put an end to the corrupt regime, reestablish the Persian true heritage, and live in peace and toler-ance with the rest of the world. Democracy and Human Rights

---

1   Zoroastrian seven guardian angels are: Ahura Mazda, angel of mighty wisdom; Mitra, angel of the sun; Mah, angel of the moon; Zam, angel of the earth; Anahita, angel of water; Atar, angel of fire; Vahay, angel of the wind.

2   Xenophon's Cyrus the Great: the arts of leadership and war/edited with and introduction by Larry Hendrick.

3   Arab Muslim invasion of Persia in 642 AD.

are the terminologies most used by this awakening generation. They are inspired by the Principles of Human Rights established by Cyrus the Great in the dawn of the Persian historical period.

Renaissance

Mason Balouchian

At the dawn of the new empire,
When kings of the four corners
In the City of the Persians
Rejoice Shah's coronation

Clad in black turban, long dolman
In disguise, Dahaka[1] rises again
Consuming the deluded brains
Turning son against father

Spreading lies and deception
Army of Satanic Guardians
Roaming the Middle Earth
Deliver terror and fear

They last four scores less,
Enlightened sons of *the Father*
With the mark of goodness on chest
Confine the Deceiver in Mt. Damavand

---

1   The mythical tyrant with snakes on his shoulder.

List of illustrations and photos:

1- Page 14: Panoramic view of the Towers of Silence in Yazd, Iran, Adobestock.com.

2- Page 69: Caravanserai at Maranjab Desert, Isfahan province, Adobestock.com.

3- Page 97: Conquest of Babylon (Antiquity), Adobestock.com.

4- Page 115: Cyrus liberates the Jewish slaves, Adobestock.com.

5- Page 151: The tomb of Cyrus the Great, Pasargad, Iran, Adobestock.com.

6- Farvahar symbol on page 6 and all the maps are illustrated by: Mason Balouchian.

Coming Soon

Novelettes, and Short Stories by
Mason Balouchian on Kindle

www.amazon.com/author/masonbalouchian

Manufactured by Amazon.ca
Bolton, ON

13075186R00099